FINANCIAL BOOT CAMP

HOW TO
AVOID AMERICA'S
FIFTEEN CONSUMER
LAND MINES

FINANCIAL BOOT CAMP

HOW TO AVOID AMERICA'S FIFTEEN CONSUMER LAND MINES

CAMP

JAMES L. PARIS

CREATION HOUSE
BOOKS ABOUT SPIRIT-LED LIVING
LAKE MARY, FLORIDA

Creation House
Strang Communications Company
600 Rinehart Road
Lake Mary, FL 32746

First printing, November 1992
Second printing, April 1993
Third printing, May 1993

To my parents, Jim and Sharon Paris.
Their story of financial hardship is the inspiration
for the writing of this book.
They are to be recognized for their triumph
over financial tragedy and their relentless
commitment to the Lord Jesus Christ.

ACKNOWLEDGMENTS

I would like to thank the following persons:
- Jennifer Polla, my writing assistant, for her hard work and dedication, which have made this book a reality;
- Creation House, specifically Walter Walker and Jerry Parsons, who have worked so diligently on this project;
- My wife, Ann, and our children, Jim and Joy, for their sacrifice in allowing me to spend hour upon hour writing;
- My colleagues J.W. Dicks and Charles Smith — these godly men will never know how much they have molded my life; and
- Greg Polla, George Holsapple, Ron Redd, Carmen Paris, Mark Moscone, Sue Darwick and Christine Singman, who have helped immensely in the completion of this book.

Contents

Tables

A s a pastor I see a lot of people who have been blindsided by financial mistakes. They have either made some poor decisions and/or incurred creeping catastrophic debt, and they are in deep trouble. And I can personally look in the mirror and see an individual who has made some bad financial decisions himself.

I wish the people I've seen in my office had known and followed the principles James Paris shares in this book. And I wish the person I see in the mirror every day had met James long ago.

As I've read through this book, I have become increasingly convinced that we Christians need a financial boot camp. We need to reevaluate the way we conduct our financial affairs. We need to examine the relationship between our faith and financial stewardship above and beyond what it means to tithe. We need to see that stewardship relates to the way we think about and spend every dollar we earn.

I am thankful to James. I know he could have written a book three times as long and much more complex. But I'm grateful that he's written this one! It's a book with principles that can be understood and applied. It's a book that can help all of us be better stewards of the resources God has given us. It's a book that can help us prevent some of the financial disasters we've witnessed and a book that can give us confidence in this important area of life.

Denny Rydberg, director
University Ministries
University Presbyterian Church
Seattle, Washington
October 1992

VICTIM TURNED ADVOCATE

Most advocates are former victims. James Brady, who was injured in the assassination attempt on former President Ronald Reagan, now lobbies for gun control legislation. The founder of Mothers Against Drunk Driving (MADD), Candy Lightner, lost a child because of an accident involving a drunk driver. Most people who are truly inspired with a life mission have had a life-changing experience. This is true in my case.

I am committed to teaching Christians how to make the most of the material possessions with which God has blessed them. My mission started at the age of fifteen in Chicago. Within moments of coming home from school one day, I learned that my father, a construction worker, had been injured at work and was at the hospital. We were shocked, but we assumed that everything would be all right. We were wrong.

During the next ten years my father underwent thirteen hospital stays and several surgeries for a lower-back injury. He could no longer work and provide for his family. The word *stress* took on a scary meaning. On at least two occasions my father could have died or been paralyzed during surgery. However, there was another type of stress that was in many ways equally damaging. This stress was financial.

Not a day would go by without some financially related problem being discussed in our home. Many times my mother would burst into tears, and my father, who held back his emotions, reacted in his own way.

Part of this tragedy was how my family was exploited by the business community. My father's employer was required by law to have workers' compensation insurance. This provides workers injured on the job with steady income as well as coverage for medical expenses related to that injury. But my father's insurance company would systematically turn off his regular benefits from time to time (almost in a predictable pattern), putting my family into a severe financial predicament. My father finally had to procure an attorney, who informed us that this was a common practice that saved money for insurance companies. This shocked me. As a young person I still believed in justice and honesty in corporate America.

The good news is that our local church was very supportive during our family crisis, which lasted for ten years. My parents paid all their bills on time, which was nothing short of a miracle. I remember that we would receive money in the mail anonymously or with a note signed simply, "A Friend." I learned two lessons from these experiences:

• God provides for His children.

• The financial community does not necessarily operate in an ethical manner.

That second lesson is not based solely on the experience with my father but has been confirmed by many clients with whom I have worked.

My life mission is to educate the Christian community on how to handle its finances wisely and invest for the future. My pursuit of financial stability for all has led to the writing of this book. It is dedicated to the millions of Christians who, like my family, have been victims of unforeseen financial dangers, the consumer land mines that can wreck lives.

A s I conduct seminars and appear on talk shows around the country, people ask me a lot of questions. Such topics as credit, home buying and investing draw the most questions. You'll find that on the chapters dealing with these popular topics, I've included some of these common questions.

However, I am going to answer now one question that is invariably asked: What is your secret? People believe that one principle is behind financial success; if they could master just that one thing, they could be successful. This may surprise you, but I do happen to believe there is one primary secret to financial success. I call it the Principle of 633.

The principle is based on Matthew 6:33 (NKJV): "Seek first the kingdom of God and His righteousness, and all these things shall be added to you." Although this book is packed with practical strategies and techniques on personal finance, they are overshadowed by the Principle of 633. The basic premise is to put God first, and He will help you take care of everything else.

I have been able to master things from personal finance to music, but one area that continues to be a struggle for me is time management. Most people who know me personally and professionally would probably not perceive this to be one of my weaknesses, but it is. I say this because I have yet to master the ability to make God the number-one priority on my calendar every day, in accordance with Matthew 6:33. The world, it seems, has already filled my day in advance, and God is noticeably absent from the agenda. Yet I know one thing is true: The more often I make God a priority, the more often He opens doors and provides for me.

Please don't misunderstand this principle as prosperity theology. I do not believe that everyone is better off with millions of dollars. God, in His infinite wisdom, meets our needs and gives to each of us various amounts of His resources to manage for Him. This responsibility is based on our commitment to taking action, our commitment to being wise and resourceful managers, and our commitment to Matthew 6:33.

Money — Root of All Evil?

Many people are guilty of misquoting Scripture on this point. "The Bible says that money is the root of all evil," they say. In reality 1 Timothy 6:10 (NKJV) says, "For the love of money is a root of all kinds of evil." It is not money that is evil but the *love* of money or a wrong attitude about money. In my financial planning organization, we teach people that money is a neutral thing. What links money with good or evil is our attitude about it and our handling of it.

Many Christians mistakenly believe that money is evil, and thus they ignore the message of this book and other materials that attempt to teach correct attitudes and the best management of money. Financial soundness or success becomes "worldly" and therefore sinful.

God has often used people who were very wealthy, such as the patriarchs Abraham, Isaac and Jacob, and the kings David and Solomon. As a reward for asking for wisdom, God said to Solomon, "I will also give you wealth, riches and honor, such as no king who was before you ever had and none after you will have" (2 Chron. 1:12). Job was a righteous man who lost great wealth only to have God restore it after a period of testing. Joseph and Moses had great wealth and were mightily used by God for the benefit of His people. Jesus' ministry was supported by wealthy Jews. The list goes on and on.

Take a hard look at your perspectives about money. Is money evil in your life because of your attitude and handling of it? Or is money merely a tool that God has given you to meet your needs and the needs of others? Can you be an example to others with your wise handling of finances?

An old chorus is titled "Jesus Be the Lord of All." The chorus points out that if He's not Lord of every *thing* in your life, then He's not Lord at all. Before you begin to work on your personal finances, you must be certain that God is number one in your life. That means more than just a salvation experience. For example, it is important to have a daily prayer schedule, a time where you can communicate with the Father, who is able to meet your every need. This is also a time when you can present to Him a list of priorities to discover whether the way you are living your life pleases Him. What is your priority? Is it Jesus Christ? Or is it money?

An easy way to discover your priorities is to look at your schedule and your checkbook. You will see very quickly where your primary assets — time and money — are going. And then you will see where your heart is.

True Success

How do you define success? The world views success as having it all — money, fame, power. You are successful if you have millions of dollars, drive an expensive car, live in an exclusive neighborhood and are physically attractive. How different is God's idea of success!

"What good will it be for a man if he gains the whole world, yet forfeits his soul?" (Matt. 16:26). God defines success as obedience to Him. This includes obedience to the Bible's frequent exhortation to be wise stewards. If the Lord gives you an income of $20,000 per year, He expects you to use that amount to the best of your ability. The same applies to the person who makes $2 million a year. God gives to each one a level of responsibility, and He expects good stewardship from each one. We want to be able to stand before God at the judgment and hear Him say, "Well done, thou good and faithful servant" (Matt. 25:21, KJV).

Teaching you good stewardship is the goal of this book. The strategies will help you make the most of your financial resources through wise investments and avoidance of scams, schemes and debt pitfalls, but the primary objective is to help you order your priorities and put God in control — of both your finances and your everyday life. That is success!

ONE

THE LAND MINE
OF COMPULSIVE
SPENDING

The foolish man spends whatever he gets.
Proverbs 21:20 (TLB)

S ome psychologists say compulsive spending is like alcoholism and other substance addictions. I believe it. I have had a firsthand perspective on lives ruined by this out-of-control behavior.

Our government has set a poor example. Congress vastly outspends the tax dollars brought in each year, leaving Americans trillions of dollars in debt. Many strategists theorize that within ten to fifteen years, if our government continues this pattern, we could be on the verge of an economic collapse. It is a very real possibility.

Many individuals are in a similar situation. The difference is that it may be only a matter of months before an individual reaches the point of financial collapse.

The principle of this chapter is this: Spend no more than you earn. You cannot outspend your income indefinitely. It will catch up with you eventually, and the results are devastating.

This chapter will tell you:

• How credit card use is destroying the finances of Christians.

• Why earning more money won't solve the problem.

• How to set up a reasonable budget.

The remainder of the book will give more details about important steps to take toward financial stability, such as getting the most out of your surplus income, avoiding excessive insurance, buying a home and reducing your taxes. At the end of some of the chapters I have included answers to the questions people ask most frequently about the topic. If you are unfamiliar with some of the terms in this book, the glossary contains easy-to-understand explanations in everyday language.

Credit Crunch

One reason that compulsive spending has become such a devastating issue for Christians in the past fifteen years is credit card abuse. In the 1950s and 1960s financial security was defined as having three to six months of income set aside in cash for emergencies (and that's still a good rule). Today the unspoken definition of financial security is having room on one or two credit cards to spend even more.

Amazingly, as the number of personal bankruptcies doubled over the past decade, banks continued to lend money irresponsibly. This is the main reason for the savings and loan failures — they lent too much money to parties who were unable or unwilling to pay it back. On the other end of the spectrum, consumers have been just as irresponsible by using more money than can be repaid.

I am critical of financial institutions and retail establishments that offer "buy now, pay later" advice and give customers credit cards charging 18 to 24 percent interest. This hardly encourages wise spending. Rather, once a customer reaches his or her credit limit, the banks or stores often increase the credit line, encouraging the customer to go further into debt. I liken this practice to that of a drug dealer, who gives out free samples in order to gain more customers by getting them hooked. As Proverbs 22:7 (RSV) accurately observes, "The borrower is the slave of the lender."

With credit being made so available, credit card indebtedness jumped from $60 billion in 1980 to more than $280 billion in 1990. This was a major cause of the doubling of the personal bankruptcies during the same period.

The slippery slope that leads to bankruptcy can be better understood by looking at the Rule of 72, which will be discussed further in another chapter. The rule says you can take any interest rate you are earning and divide it into seventy-two to learn how long it will take your money to double. Money earning 12 percent a year, for example, will double in six years.

This rule also works in reverse. Take the interest rate you are *paying* on debts and divide it into seventy-two. This will give you the number of years it will take for your *debt* to double. Take a credit card charging 24 percent interest, as some department store cards do. Divide twenty-four into seventy-two, and you'll see that once every three years your debt on that credit card will double unless you are paying it off. According to the national media, 85 percent of Americans allow their credit card balances to roll over each month without reducing the balance — they simply make the negligible minimum payment and keep using the card, so they never gain ground.

More Money Isn't the Answer

I have worked with individuals who have won a major

lottery or received large inheritances or insurance settlements, and, unfortunately, their stories are similar. Prior to receiving the money, they genuinely feel that they will be responsible with it. They make investment plans. Several even go to a financial planner and have an investment portfolio developed. Relatives warn them to be careful with the money.

Once the money is received, the person says, Well, there are a few things I want. Maybe it's a car, improvements to his home, the purchase of a new home or perhaps an expensive vacation. But a certain amount of the money is untouchable, he says. It will definitely be invested. Over months, and then years, he procrastinates on investing and continues to touch the untouchable sum. In many cases the individual will go through thousands of dollars and end up with little to show for it.

I've read stories of lottery winners. Many were receiving their money in intervals — say, $50,000 per year for twenty years. However, friends and relatives assumed they had received the entire amount in a lump sum. Thus, these friends also assumed the winners would pay for dinners out, drive new cars, buy bigger houses, and so on. The winners' egos inflated to the point where they needed to keep up the façade of being millionaires. Some winners were bankrupt after receiving their final checks.

I have never met anyone who was not able to outspend his or her income. I have worked with doctors and lawyers whose annual incomes are over $500,000 to try to help them spend within their means and avoid bankruptcy. When I tell this story at my seminars, people don't believe me. So I tell them to look at their current bills and add a zero to each one. The $1,000 mortgage payment becomes $10,000; the $350 car payment becomes $3,500. Then I explain that this is the dilemma of the "rich." They have greater incomes, but their expenditures are higher as they try to maintain a certain life-style.

If you get nothing more from this chapter, retain this: *Unless you learn to live within your current means, it makes no difference what your income is.* As your income increases, so will your spending. Those who refuse to get spending under control face a discipline issue, which is essentially a spiritual problem. Part of this stems from self-image. In what do you place your confidence? Is it the security of being a child of God, loved by Him unconditionally? Is it from the nice home with the outrageous mortgage payment? Or the expensive car that drains your cash flow? We are all guilty of this to some extent — whether it is the child's desire for new clothes for school to impress her friends or the pastor who wants a bigger church building to impress his colleagues.

There is nothing inherently wrong with having nice things. The problem develops when our need for things is placed above our need to be responsible to the Lord and to our families with our income. Within the church today, financial irresponsibility is the most destructive force. Compulsive spending is a psychological illness Satan uses to harm people, just as he does with other addictions. Far more people are affected by the sin of compulsive spending than are being destroyed by drugs and alcohol.

Advertising plays an insidious role in this disease. Often I find myself agreeing with a television commercial, thinking, Yes, it would be great if I could have that product. It would solve all my problems. Americans view and hear thousands of advertisements each year, and Madison Avenue uses every clever approach to manipulate our minds.

Cash Flow

A relative of mine describes his perpetual state of no money as "cash flow problems." There are only two ways to solve cash flow problems. One is to increase what's flowing in — your income. The second is to decrease what's flowing out — your spending. The most realistic solution is a combination of the two because we know that increasing our income usually causes us to increase spending as well.

Most people, if they were honest, could find fat in their monthly spending that they could eliminate to decrease the outflow of cash. They could brownbag their lunches instead of eating out during the week. They could quit smoking. They could buy fuel-efficient cars and spend less on gasoline.

The first thing to do is to determine where your money goes. Many people have no idea. They just know what income they get is not enough. A simple way to learn your spending habits is to carry a small notebook for four to six weeks. Write down every expenditure, even if it is a 50-cent candy bar. At the end of the period, analyze your spending by categorizing the expenditures. Some people are amazed to learn they are spending $30 or $40 a month on potato chips and sodas. But with that new understanding of their spending patterns, they can make some adjustments.

Next, set up a realistic budget. This may seem like a lot of trouble, but it is the easy part. The hard part is living by it. A basic work sheet to help you get started is included in this chapter (see table 1 on page 26). When you have completed it, compare your total income to your total expenses. If your expenses exceed your income, then *cut your expenses*. Next, strive to achieve a good balance between your saving and spending, as I will explain in the next section.

Table 1
Monthly Budget Work Sheet

Month of _____, 19 _____

Monthly Income:
    Salaries   _____
    Other   _____

    Total Income   _____

Monthly Expenses:
    Savings   _____
    Food   _____
    Rent/Mortgage   _____
    Electricity   _____
    Telephone   _____
    Other Utilities   _____
    Household Expense   _____
    Auto Expense   _____
    Insurance   _____
    Loans   _____
    Education   _____
    Clothing   _____
    Laundry, Cleaning   _____
    Personal Care   _____
    Entertainment   _____
    Gifts   _____
    Miscellaneous   _____

Tax-Deductible Expenses:
    Withholding Taxes   _____
    Medical Expenses   _____
    Contributions   _____
    Home Loan Interest   _____
    Child Care   _____
    Miscellaneous   _____

    Total Expenses   _____

60 Percent Is Enough

There is no right or wrong budget. It is an individual or family decision. However, I like to use the rule *60 percent is enough*. This means you should live on no more than 60 percent of your gross income. I know 60 percent doesn't sound like much, but let me explain.

Ten percent of your income should be tithed — that is, given away to your church or other charitable causes — and 10 percent should be placed into a savings plan. On average, another 20 percent of your income will be given to pay taxes. This leaves 60 percent of your gross income for all other expenses. Too many Americans are outspending their income and plunging into debt because they do not plan for these standard expenditures. You may think at first that it is impossible to live on 60 percent of your income, but you are setting yourself up for great problems in the future if you overspend that amount.

In summary, the three mandatory considerations for setting up your budget are:

• Tithing 10 percent of your income to the Lord.

• Saving 10 percent for the future — for children's education, retirement and emergency reserves.

• Paying taxes (approximately 20 percent).

Beyond these requirements, each individual's spending patterns will be different. For example, a single person spends more money on dining out and entertainment than a married person, and that is justified. Families will spend more on a home than single individuals will. Net spendable income will vary from person to person, but the budgetary concept remains the same.

Once you form a budget, how do you stick to it? If you are having a hard time sticking to a budget, try the envelope system. Label an envelope for each budget category. If you have decided that $100 per month will be allocated for clothing, place $100 in that clothing envelope. When you go shopping for clothes, take that envelope. Any leftover money stays in the envelope. Once that envelope is empty, there should be no further expenditures for clothing that month. It may seem overly rigid, but this is how you should adhere to your budget if you are having trouble making ends meet.

Money is a finite commodity — there is not an unlimited supply. We must live our lives with this realization. Spiritual and financial maturity is the goal. When you can wait until you have the cash to make a purchase, you have learned self-discipline. A simple little phrase I learned as a child goes like this:

> Use it up,
> Wear it out,
> Make it do or
> Do without.

Some wise words to live by. We all have wants, and there is nothing necessarily evil about having them. It's part of being alive. I believe people should enjoy this life, and part of the enjoyment comes from "toys" we acquire. Remember to make God a part of your budget plan, as He can still work miracles for you. Commit your dreams and goals to the Lord because perhaps He has a different plan to allow you to have some of the things you would like.

Consumer Tips

I asked some "professional shoppers," including my wife, to contribute some tips for saving money. Here goes:

Clothing. Try out some consignment or secondhand shops. Many times you can find beautiful clothes at a fraction of their original cost. You can even take your better clothes to these shops when you become weary of them. They will be sold for you, and you will receive a percentage of the sales price.

Food and Drugs. It is normally less expensive to cook and bake using ingredients from scratch rather than buying prepared or prepackaged products. Buy a freezer and buy meats, vegetables and other products in bulk, freezing the portions you do not plan to use immediately.

Ask the pharmacist for the generic brand of prescription drugs, especially if your doctor has not specified a certain brand on the prescription. Also, the generic brands of over-the-counter medications such as aspirin and cold remedies have the same ingredients as the heavily advertised brands and are much less expensive.

Coupons. Many products can be purchased at a discount by using coupons. Some general rules: Check the newspaper regularly for coupons, and clip only those for products you use. Use a filing system to sort the coupons by category, such as cereals, drinks, cookies/snacks and the like, and keep them in a file box or wallet. Sort through them periodically to throw out the expired ones. Ask friends or relatives to collect certain coupons you use frequently for which they have no use, such as diaper coupons.

If you are not brand-conscious on a particular item, such as dish soap, collect all the coupons for this product and buy the one which happens to be cheapest at the time of purchase. For coupon items, shop at the stores that double the face value of the coupon to get the lowest price. Note, however, that these stores normally make up for the coupon-doubling by raising the prices of many other goods, so buy only your coupon items at these stores. Finally, decide which rebate offers are worth the time and stamps it takes to utilize them.

Entertainment. Utilize your public library when looking

for a good book, rather than buying it at the bookstore. If possible, attend movies during the daytime to get the matinee rate, rather than paying full price in the evening. Pack a picnic lunch for an outing with the family, rather than paying too much at the fast-food places. Check on condominium rentals rather than hotels for vacations. Many times you can rent an entire house or condo for the price of a hotel room.

Gifts. The long summer months provide a wonderful opportunity to prepare for Christmas by making gifts, even enlisting the older children. In this way you save money as well as avoid the mad rush in December, and you teach the joy of giving and creativity to your children. (No, you don't have to be an artist!) Some ideas for gifts include:

• Decorated clothing, such as painted T-shirts.
• Place mats. Make them with cards and laminate them, or cover them with contact paper.
• Jewelry. There are free workshops at craft stores and many books on this subject.
• Picture frames. Decorate inexpensive frames and personalize them by adding a favorite photo.
• Christmas tree ornaments.
• Pottery (for you talented folks).
• Videos. During the year, if you have a video camcorder, record special events and fun times. It makes a great gift for grandparents.

Garage Sales. Have a garage sale periodically. We all accumulate stuff that we no longer need or want. As the saying goes, "One man's trash is another man's treasure." You will be amazed at the money you can make at these sales. Advertise your sale in the local paper and get several neighbors involved for an even bigger sale, thus attracting more buyers. Have a few big items to sell, rather than all small items. Be sure to call your city or county court house to see whether you need to purchase a permit for the sale.

Increasing Income

So far my emphasis has been on ways to decrease spending. Now let's talk about the other side of cash flow — increasing income. People say, "Jim, there is absolutely no way I can increase my income. My employer is not giving raises this year."

Such thinking is too narrow. There are several ways to increase income outside of your present job. Some are simple; some are more complicated. Most of us Americans look for the easy way, the simple solution. However, it takes time to get into too much debt, and it takes time and effort to get out of debt and live within one's means.

Maybe you are close to finishing a college degree or certification that would give you the added education to get a promotion or command a higher salary. Take the steps to finish that education.

Consider starting your own business. This is not as insurmountable as it sounds. One couple I knew loved children, and I counseled them to start a small toy business at a flea market. The business is now generating thousands of dollars in profit, and it is something they thoroughly enjoy. I know avid fishermen who run charters and golfers who give lessons and sell golf equipment.

By using your hobby, you can often create outstanding business ideas and take advantage of the many tax write-offs that small businesses enjoy. There are roughly twenty-five tax deductions afforded the small businessman that are not available to the salaried worker. Often small business owners pay less in taxes than employees because the government has given great incentives to starting a small business. To find out more about these deductions, the IRS has a free brochure, publication 334, which you can get by calling the IRS at (800) 829-3676.

Summary

As we close this chapter, spend a moment in prayer. Ask the Lord to work in your life in this area, to forgive you for any excess spending and to protect you from the sickness and sin of compulsive spending. You need to have mastered the foundational principle of spending no more than you earn if you plan to maximize the benefits from the other strategies discussed in this book.

Keep your eyes and ears open. Realize that advertisers are trying to make you feel insecure and trying to convince you that a certain product will make you happy. Be one step ahead of them by planning expenditures wisely and by following a budget. The future of your family's financial security is at stake. And remember, material possessions and worldly experiences will not bring you happiness. Only confidence in your relationship with Jesus Christ brings fulfillment.

Questions

Practical Budgets

Question: My husband and I agree we should be on a budget. The problem is that we've never stuck by any of the budgets we have ever created. We have just about given up. Can you help us?

Answer: The problem with most budgets is that they are not practical, meaning that they are not easy to live on. What most people put together as a budget is simply a piece of paper with all of their expenditures itemized. Once that is completed, they put it in their drawer, never to look at it again. It is very important to create a system for enforcing the budget. The envelope system, discussed in this chapter, works very well for introducing your budget to reality.

For some people, credit cards (to be discussed in the next chapter) are their greatest budget adversaries. For example, if you're a person who eats out every day and you use a credit card, chances are you are not keeping track of how much you're spending. So if your budget allocates $25 a week for lunch, then what would probably be more effective is to give yourself $25 in cash every Monday. Now, if on Thursday you have no money left, what do you do? No, you don't go to the auto-teller machine and get more money out. The answer is that you bring a brown-bag lunch until next Monday.

You must learn how to live within your means. If you can't do that, you will stay in an endless cycle of outspending your income.

TWO

THE LAND MINE
OF CREDIT

The borrower is the slave of the lender.
Proverbs 22:7 (TLB)

S hould a Christian borrow money? We get an assort-
ment of opinions on this from the counselors and
theologians of today. Some of these opinions have a
biblical base; others do not.

I am a firm believer that Christians may use debt to their
advantage, provided it is used wisely. As we saw in the last
chapter, many Americans have gotten themselves into
financial bondage with the misuse of credit.

Debt and Stewardship

A young woman approached me after a television interview in Chicago in which I had shared my views on credit.
She said, "Wait a minute. You said during the interview
that Christians can have debt. I disagree. I don't think it's

right biblically for a Christian to have any debt."

I asked her if she lived in a home on which there was a mortgage. She said yes. She also admitted to having financed the purchase of her automobile. I asked her how she would have been able to buy her home or her car without using debt. She acknowledged that it would not have been possible.

With the average price of a new automobile over $17,000 and the average price of a home in the United States over $118,000, it is obvious why most of us are unable to purchase shelter or transportation outright. Many Christians who say that Scripture commands that we should never incur debt will often make allowances for houses and automobiles. The Bible's truths are unbending, however. If these people truly believe that the Bible forbids the use of credit, then this should extend to all purchases.

The proper use of credit can be good stewardship. For example, it is a waste of your money to be paying rent when for roughly the same amount of dollars you could be paying on a mortgage and building equity in a property you will someday own.

Psalm 37:21 says, "The wicked borrow and do not repay." Notice that verse does not say only, "The wicked borrow." Rather, the ungodly action is the refusal to repay what has been borrowed.

Romans 13:7-8 says, "Give everyone what you owe him: if you owe taxes, pay taxes; if revenue, then revenue; if respect, then respect; if honor, then honor. Let no debt remain outstanding, except the continuing debt to love one another, for he who loves his fellowman has fulfilled the law."

I believe it is a mistake to construe these verses to be forbidding the use of credit on the part of the believer. The emphasis seems to be on honoring our commitments in a timely fashion and on never exhausting the capacity to give love. At the same time, many verses warn of the dangers involved in the abuse of credit. We would be wise to read all the Bible's references to debt.

Credit can be one of the most powerful tools, and at the same time it can cause financial ruin if not used properly. Our country is now recognized for two dubious financial hallmarks: Americans are the most leveraged (propped up with borrowed money) people in the world, and we save the least amount of our income.

Even our government has become overwhelmed with debt — currently at $4 trillion. Rarely does a political debate go by without the national debt being discussed. But is credit in and of itself bad? Absolutely not. However, the use of credit does carry with it a great degree of responsibility.

Credit card companies are increasing their marketing efforts to include gimmicks, like extended warranties on products purchased with their card. There is even a card that "pays you cash back." Guess whose money it pays you. Department stores have what amounts to street barkers positioned at every entrance to solicit you to sign up for their credit cards. Our "buy now, pay later" society is start- ing to feel the credit crunch as "buy now" becomes past tense and "pay later" becomes present tense. Without a doubt, credit is the perfect example of the proverbial dou- ble-edged sword that cuts both ways.

Your Credit Report

I have had people tell me they don't use credit, and therefore they don't need a credit rating. However, a credit rating is very important at certain times. If you wish to rent an apartment, lease or buy a car, or obtain a home mort- gage, you will need to have a credit rating. Many employ- ers now request copies of a prospective employee's credit file because it serves as a type of objective character reference. A bad credit file will follow you into many areas of your life. Bad marks can remain on a credit report for seven to ten years. It is also a poor witness to the secular community when a Christian refuses to repay his or her debts.

How are these credit files established? Many people ask me about credit bureaus, which build these files. Some people think these bureaus are somehow linked to the government, namely the Internal Revenue Service. But they aren't. Credit bureaus are private organizations that collect data on individuals and provide that information to members of their organizations, such as retailers and banks.

When you use a form of credit, such as a student loan or a credit card, you are given goods and services up front with the agreement that you will pay later. When you make payments to the lender, that entity reports to a credit bureau on how you are performing, based on your agreement. If you pay on time, that information is relayed to the credit bureau. If you are thirty days late or ninety days late or refuse to repay the loan altogether, that information is also relayed to the credit bureau.

Other businesses belonging to this credit bureau can receive this information about your payment history. It aids them in determining whether or not they wish to extend credit to you.

There are laws governing how this information can be used, and you have some basic rights under the Fair Credit Reporting Act. First and foremost, you have the right to obtain a copy of your credit report to see what information has been supplied about your payment history. Getting a copy is easier than you may think. The Fair Credit Reporting Act entitles you to a *free* copy of your credit report any time you are denied credit based on the information in your report. If you have not been denied credit, a fee of $15 to $20 is required. There are three major credit bureaus: Trans

Union, TRW and Equifax, and you may contact them at the following addresses and phone numbers.

Equifax Credit Information Service Center
P.O. Box 740241
Atlanta, GA 30374-0241
(404) 612-3114

Trans Union Credit
P.O. Box 8070
North Olmsted, OH 44070
(316) 263-0166

TRW Credit Services
P.O. Box 749029
Dallas, TX 75374
(214) 235-1200

I recommend getting a copy of your credit report once or twice a year. Sometimes information that does not belong to you will appear on your report, especially if you have a common name such as John Smith. This problem is more common than you might imagine. At one of my seminars more than 10 percent of the people raised their hands when asked, "Have you ever had incorrect information show up on your credit file?"

Once you have received your credit report, it is easy to determine the quality of your credit. You have the right to:

• *Dispute any incorrect information and have it removed.* Write a letter to the credit bureau, explaining the incorrect data. It is then investigated by the credit bureau. If the company reporting the information cannot prove the bad data, then that information must be removed from your report within thirty days.

• *Enclose a written response (limited to one hundred*

words) to explain circumstances beyond your control that resulted in derogatory credit information. Perhaps you were hospitalized, which caused you to be late on some payments. This statement will be attached to your file.

• *Have positive credit information added to your file if it is missing.* If you notice that some good credit history never got picked up, put it in writing to the bureau, and they will add it.

• *Use a small claims court to resolve disputes with the credit bureau.* This is usually when the credit bureau refuses to correct your file.

The Federal Trade Commission regulates the credit bureaus. If a bureau is not cooperating with you, contact the FTC in Washington, D.C., at (202) 326-3128. Contacts for other FTC offices may be found in appendix A, and contacts for state attorney general offices can be found in appendix B.

I would recommend that before you apply for a loan, call the lending institution you plan to use and ask them which credit reporting agency they use. Then call this agency and request a copy of your credit report. There is nothing worse than applying for a loan and being embarrassed by your credit file when you could have had that information in advance.

If you have no credit history or bad credit, you need to start building a positive history. Do not believe advertisements where companies claim to wipe out bad credit histories — these companies charge huge fees for taking steps that you can do for free.

An easy way to begin establishing good credit is to deposit $500 or $1,000 with a bank and then ask them for a loan for the same amount. They will hold your deposit as collateral while you pay off the loan. Once you have paid off this loan, go to another bank and do the same thing. This process will begin to build positive information on your credit file.

A second way of establishing good credit is with a secured credit card, either a Visa or MasterCard. A secured credit card requires you to make a deposit equal to the amount of credit that will be made available to you, usually $300 to $500. These credit cards look exactly like unsecured cards — only you and the bank will know that the line of credit is secured. As you charge items and make timely payments, your positive actions will show up on your credit file.

Bankruptcy

Bankruptcy is discussed in a later chapter, but I want to make clear that incorrect use of credit is so serious that it is a cause of many bankruptcies. In the bankruptcy chapter I explain how there are two types of bankruptcy: a total discharging of debts called liquidation, where the money is not repaid; and reorganization of debts, where a systematic repayment over three to five years begins.

Reorganization is the more Christian approach because you have the intention to pay back your debts. Remember, those who borrow and refuse to pay back are wicked, both in the eyes of God and the eyes of the world. We, as Christians, are called to be responsible. I know several people who liquidated all their debts through bankruptcy but felt compelled by the Holy Spirit to repay their creditors anyway. They eventually did so, even though they were not legally obligated.

Summary

Do not take my comments about building a positive credit history to mean that I am encouraging you to get a lot of credit and use it to the hilt. Credit can be a powerful tool to buy your next home or your next automobile or even to start a small business. But it must be used wisely. It is in your best interest to guard your credit file very jealously because even employers have access to this information. Our integrity as Christians is also very important, as we witness how meaningful Christ is to us through our stewardship of sums great and small.

In appendix C you will find sources of credit cards which, at this writing, had the best rates and terms in the country. Though conditions change, these sources have historically been leaders in good credit terms, some with low rates, some with no annual fees, some with both.

Questions

Debt Counseling

Question: Is there anywhere I can go to get counseling on managing my debt?

Answer: I highly recommend the Consumer Credit Counseling Service. CCCS is a nonprofit group that helps consumers who are in financial straits. The group will help you set up a budget and teach you basic money management principles. Also, in more extenuating circumstances, they will help negotiate with your creditors. This may lead to a lower interest rate on your debts or a more lengthy pay-back period to try to work out some of your problems. To find your local CCCS, look in the telephone directory's white pages. Almost every major city has one.

Additionally, many churches now provide financial counseling. This does not have to come from a full-time staff member. Many times trained laymen, as a ministry to their church, provide financial counseling. It is very important to get outside assistance when your circumstances require it.

Credit History Repair

Question: Some people say that my credit history will follow me for the rest of my life. Is that true?

Answer: No. The information on a credit report must by cycled off every seven years. However, in the case of personal bankruptcy, it will stay on your report for as long as ten years. Additionally, although bankruptcy will come off your credit file after ten years, many lenders are now asking in loan applications, "Have you *ever* filed for bankruptcy?" Even though your ten years have passed, you are expected to reveal your bankruptcy upon request.

So this may affect you for the rest of your life, though it doesn't mean that you'll never be able to get another loan. In fact, most people find that after going through a bankruptcy, they were able to obtain major credit cards and get back into the credit game in two or three years. Your credit will never be the same after a bankruptcy, but you can improve it to the degree that you can get automobile loans, credit cards and, after a number of years of working to repair that credit, even a mortgage.

Low-Interest-Rate Credit Cards

Question: Is it more difficult to qualify for a low-interest-rate credit card than for a high-interest-rate credit card?

Answer: Yes, but only slightly. The banks offering low-interest-rate credit cards typically approve more than 65 percent of the people applying — a very fair rate. Obviously, since they do have the supply and demand scale tipped in their favor, they can use that as an opportunity to choose people with better credit ratings and payment histories. However, if you're turned down by one firm that issues low-interest-rate credit cards, don't be afraid simply to fill out an application for another. One bank's criteria may differ from another's.

Liquidating High-Rate Debt

Question: Does it make sense to use low-interest credit cards as a source of cash to pay off other high-interest-rate debt, like high-interest-rate credit cards?

Answer: Absolutely! Let's say that you are paying 24 percent on one card's debt. You may very easily find a credit card with an interest rate between 10 and 11 percent. By getting the low-interest-rate credit card, taking a cash advance on the low-rate card and paying off the high-interest debt, you can save as much as 40 percent on your monthly payments.

Incorrect Credit Card Charges

Question: What can I do if I find an incorrect charge on my credit card statement?

Answer: The Fair Credit Billing Act of 1975 allows you to dispute any incorrect billing information on your credit card statement. Simply send the credit card company a letter explaining the error, and they will then investigate it with the merchant. The burden of proof is on the merchant, not on you. Additionally, you are not required to pay any amount that is placed in dispute until the matter is resolved. This also applies to overcharges, defective merchandise received, and so forth. If you do not get cooperation from your credit card company, it may be necessary for you to contact the Federal Trade Commission (see appendix A).

THREE

THE LAND MINE OF THE AUTO PURCHASE

*They imported a chariot from Egypt for
six hundred shekels of silver.*
2 Chronicles 1:17

A hotbed of political controversy involves the quality of domestic versus foreign automobiles. As you can see from the above verse, importing vehicles is not a new phenomenon. Yet for the consumer, greater than the issue of foreign versus domestic is the need for wisdom when buying a car.

The average American will buy a new car every five to six years. The median cost of automobiles sold as new is more than $17,000. This is considered the second largest purchase most of us will make in our lifetime, one in which we need to take great care.

Most people have no idea how to go into an automobile dealership and get a good deal. I am going to teach you how to approach this purchase wisely. I will also talk about dealer add-ons and rip-off schemes that are pure profit schemes for the dealer. Avoid them.

Dealership Games

"Jim, I just got a great deal on a new car," I'm often told. I ask how they know it was such a good deal, and they tell me how they negotiated and negotiated, the salesman seemed unhappy, and they left with the feeling that they put the dealership through the ringer.

The truth is that they have experienced the game of selling an automobile. Everyone who purchases a new car leaves the automobile dealership under the impression that they won and the dealer lost because the sales department plans it that way. It's part of the presentation. You, therefore, must base your decision on facts and the determination to buy at a certain price, not on emotion or on the dealership's game.

First, you must have an automobile model and price in mind. If you are starting without a specific model, begin to narrow your search by talking with friends and reading *Consumer Reports* and other consumer magazines. These magazines give detailed reports on critical factors such as engine performance, mileage, handling and repair history (for older cars). Make some cursory trips to new and used car dealers to get a general idea of what you can get for your money.

Second, when you have settled on one or two models, find out the basic dealer cost. To get the model's cost, I recommend the following, usually available at bookstores:

• *NADA Yellow Book.* This is a pricing guide for new and used cars.

• *Kelly Blue Book.* This book gives you the new car price and the used car price for all makes, going back about five years per model.

• *Consumer Reports Buying Guide.* This book details the

track record of maintenance and performance for most makes and models of automobiles.

There are also new car pricing services that you can utilize to find out the actual dealer cost of the automobile. For less than $15 you can get a quote on a specific car from Consumer Reports Auto Price Service, Box 8005, Novi, MI 48376. Check consumer magazines for other sources.

Also, if you are interested in a specific automobile, you might want to locate one at a rental agency and rent it for a week. This will give you a true feel for the vehicle with no pressure from a salesman.

Using these resources is crucial. Unless you know the wholesale cost of the automobile, you have no information from which to negotiate and make a wise purchase, and you end up as a prime target for dealership sales techniques.

Let's say reference materials show you that the new van you like has a "dealer cost" of $18,000. Most likely, when you go to the dealership you will find a sticker price of $20,000 to $21,000. I put dealer cost in quotations because even if you were able to purchase this van for $18,000, the dealer would still make some profit because that "cost" usually has built-in bonuses or rebates that the dealer will receive from the factory.

Please understand that I believe the auto dealer deserves to make a profit. Dealers perform a valuable service and should be compensated for their efforts in bringing the latest automobiles to your area. However, there are so many schemes entrenched into the system that the more informed you are as a purchaser, the better deal you will make.

Most automobile sticker prices can be reduced 15 to 20 percent through negotiation. The dealership marks up the price of the car by this margin. They know that you plan to bargain for a lower price. The process is similar to the real estate business, where a seller inflates the price, knowing that a buyer will try to bring down the purchase price. Keep this in mind as you go to a dealership and shoot for a 15 percent decrease in price. To figure from the other end, you should expect to pay a price that is about 4 percent over the dealer cost that you determined from your research. Don't get sidetracked by salespeople trying to justify their higher cost with line items such as transportation or preparation. The dealer cost should incorporate those expenses.

At the dealership, look on the driver's-side door jamb to locate a manufacturer's plate. This plate will indicate in what month the car was manufactured. If the automobile is four to five months old, the dealer has not been able to move this car and will probably be very interested in selling because he pays interest on the unsold cars on his lot.

Try to shop for a new car at the end of the month. Salespeople generally work on quotas, and they are more likely to negotiate with you toward the end of the month in order to meet their sales quota. As for the best time of year to shop, some people say the early fall is advantageous because dealers are trying to move out the previous year's models to make room for the new ones coming in. Other people say to wait until later because new cars often get overstocked, and rebates will begin to surface. I'm not sure there is a best time of year to buy a car, but the principles outlined here will work twelve months out of the year.

Stick to your facts and information. Don't be bullied by such tactics as the salesperson bringing in the manager to debate you on price. Car buying can be a very methodical exercise if you keep your emotions in check. This includes the need for you to refrain from showing excitement over a particular auto as well as being wary of falling victim to the manipulation that salespeople and managers practice as masters of their trade.

Add-on Products

Once you agree upon a price, you will be ushered into an office to fill out paperwork and possibly arrange financing. The finance manager's job is twofold — to help you finish paperwork and/or arrange for financing and to sell you add-on products. He is normally paid a commission based on what he sells you. The following are some add-ons to avoid:

Extended Warranties

Extended warranties are one of the biggest profit-makers for the dealership. They are largely unnecessary because many manufacturers are offering three- to five-year warranties or "bumper-to-bumper" type policies, which are part of the original purchase price of the vehicle. Therefore, buying a second warranty gives you unnecessary duplicate coverage. The second problem with extended warranty services is that they, unlike a manufacturer's warranty, are sometimes difficult to collect on. Finally, the warranties are usually extremely overpriced.

Credit Life Insurance

Should you die during the life of the car loan, credit life insurance guarantees that the outstanding balance would be paid off. It sounds like a fantastic deal. However, the problem is that the insurance is overpriced by about *800 percent*, which means that you could buy the same amount of term life insurance for a fraction of the cost. In fact, a good term insurance policy (discussed in the insurance chapter) should be purchased to cover these and other debts you might have in existence upon your demise as well as provide replacement income to take care of family members.

Rustproofing

Most automobiles come complete with a rust-resistant coating from the factory. In addition, most warranties include a three- to five-year (or longer) coverage for this problem. Therefore, rustproofing from the dealer would be a duplicate service, although it would give the dealer a nice bonus.

Fabric Protection

You can be charged $200 to $300 for a coating to be applied to the interior fabric. This is tempting to parents of small children, who have a tendency to spill food and drinks. However, in most cases you can save a great deal of money by going to an auto supply store, buying the chemical in a spray can and doing the treatment yourself.

New or Used?

I'm often asked whether it's better to purchase a new car or to find a good deal on a used car. In general, buying a car which is one to two years old is the best value because most of the early, rapid depreciation has occurred.

However, my opinion is being tempered by such new offerings as Chrysler's seven-year, seventy-thousand-mile warranty on new cars.

If you plan to keep an automobile for longer than five years, it may be to your advantage to buy a new car so that you can get the manufacturer's warranty.

If you are adept at picking a good used car (usually only one previous owner is desirable), and you do not have the money for a new car, then a used car may be for you. If you are handy with fixing mechanical problems, that is one further reason to consider a used car. Why spend hundreds of extra dollars in depreciation on a new car when you can find a good used car value and repair any minor problems that may occur? Also, sometimes a dealer will offer a warranty on a car that is one to two years old, and therefore a used car makes sense.

A common mistake is to buy automobiles too frequently. This is one of the fastest ways to lose money. Plan to purchase an automobile that you will enjoy five to seven years or longer. You will get the most for your money by keeping a vehicle at least this length of time.

Selling the Old Car Yourself or Trading It In

Some people insist that the only way to sell your old car is to do it yourself through newspaper classified ads. They claim that an automobile dealer will not give you a fair price if you trade it in. Realize that if you advertise your vehicle, in addition to the cost of your ad, you will have the time investment of many telephone calls and appointments.

I happen to like the convenience of trading in a vehicle at the time of purchasing a new vehicle. The only way to do this and receive a fair price, however, is to arm yourself with both the dealer cost on the new car you are buying and the Blue Book value on your old car. By having both pieces of information at your fingertips, you will assure yourself that the dealer is not boosting the price of the new car to accommodate a good trade-in price on the old, nor is he offering you too little for the old car.

Buying Government-seized Vehicles

For those of you who are really ambitious and have the time to invest, buying an automobile at an auction after it has been seized by the government may be your best route.

Although it is obvious that the ads in the classifieds that shout, "Buy a Jeep from the government for $1!" are an exaggeration, you can buy automobiles at attractive discounts through this method.

Here are the organizations to contact about these auctions:

U.S. General Services Administration
Eighteenth and F Streets NW
Washington, DC 20405
(202) 708-5082

Internal Revenue Service
IRS National Hotline
(800) 829-1040

U.S. Marshals' Service
Seized Assets Division
Department of Justice
Constitution Avenue and John Marshall Place NW
Washington, DC 20530
(202) 633-1750

Contact your local and county government offices as well because these organizations also seize property and sell it at auctions.

Insurance Considerations

Call your auto insurance company prior to the purchase of an automobile. Ask them the rate for insuring the particular vehicle you wish to buy. Automobiles are rated differently for reasons of repair expense. For example, it costs more to repair a Mercedes than a Chevy. Also, models that are stolen more often than others cost more to insure. See the insurance chapter for additional information.

Financing

Because of the price of automobiles today, most of us cannot afford to pay cash for a vehicle. It is very important to get proper financing for this purchase in order to keep your monthly costs to a minimum.

Go to the bank or credit union where you do business. They will most likely have competitive rates. Dealers obtain financing from lenders for the automobiles on their lots and then mark up that interest rate to make a profit. For instance, the bank may charge the dealer 11 percent, and he will offer you a loan at 13 percent, with that extra 2 percent being called the "spread."

When you go to your lending institution, ask for a simple interest loan. This is the most favorable form of financing for the consumer. Financing arrangements to avoid include compounding interest loans and Rule of 78 loans.

Suppose you decide to trade in the car before it is paid for. If you have been making monthly payments on a Rule of 78 or add-on loan, you will find that the majority of the principal balance is still unpaid. You will possibly owe more on the car than it is presently worth! This is known as being upside down on the loan.

With a simple interest loan you are almost sure to be protected from this situation. You will make a partial principal payment each month, along with the interest payment, so that your equity in the car grows with time.

The auto industry uses the term *strip note* to describe a loan with no add-ons, such as credit life insurance. By using this term with the finance manager, he will understand that you wish for a loan with no extras.

Finance a car for no more than three to four years, preferably three years. If you are one of those who like to purchase automobiles frequently, you will go deeper and deeper into debt by trading in cars with outstanding principal balances on them. My recommendation is to keep the car long enough to pay off the loan and then continue making car payments to yourself, putting the money aside in an interest-bearing investment so that eventually you will be able to buy an automobile with cash and save hundreds of dollars in interest.

If you are a home owner you have yet another option for financing a car. You can go to the bank and open a home equity line of credit, which is a second mortgage on your home. Depending on the value of your home, you will probably qualify for enough credit to write a check for a new car.

There are two benefits to doing this. One is that the interest paid on home loans is tax deductible. The second is that you can work out your own payment schedule as long as you are meeting the minimum monthly payment.

There are also two problems. One is that if you lack self-discipline, you could let the flexible repayment drag out over too many years, thereby paying hundreds of dollars more in interest than you should have to. Second, if your lack of self-discipline is extreme or if a job layoff or other financial tragedy strikes, you risk losing your home because it is the collateral backing up your loan.

What Size Car?

Buy an automobile based on your probable future needs, not your current needs. I made the mistake of buying a Honda Accord for my wife prior to our having a family. Within two years of buying that car, we had two children, which made the Accord very impractical. I had to take a loss on that automobile when I sold it to buy a minivan because the Accord was still relatively new. Had I bought for the future, I would have purchased a larger vehicle than the Accord.

If you are a young couple and anticipate having a family in the near future, that cute little convertible won't be the best value. I have seen many friends trade in tiny cars once the car seats and diaper bags became a part of their traveling equipment.

Summary

Determine the automobile you are interested in and get the facts on both its track record and the dealer's wholesale price. Avoid buying add-on products and obtain financing from your own bank or a lending institution in your area, making sure that it is a simple interest loan. Make sure the car you buy will fit your future needs.

Finally, stop, think and pray before you buy a new car. It is a big investment and a large commitment financially. Do you really need a new car right now? Are you motivated by true need or by self-centered considerations, such as prestige or greed? Would a used car do? Could you lower your standards enough to pay cash and avoid that monthly car note? Or could you avoid that loan by waiting a year or two and saving that money you would otherwise pay — with interest — on a note?

Maybe you can scratch the "new car itch" by taking your present auto to a detail shop, having its interior cleaned and having that new car smell sprayed inside. Make the Lord part of this decision in order to make the best choice for your financial well-being.

Questions

Saving to Buy a Car

Question: When you talk about planning for the future, you talk about long-term goals, such as retirement planning or funding a college education. Can these same principles be used for short-term goals, such as buying a car in three years?

Answer: Absolutely! The principles will work whether you're saving for something over a one-year period or a fifty-year period. The concept is simple. Decide what the goal is. Create a monthly plan to reach that goal. Follow the plan, even if your time frame is very short, such as one to three years.

The only difference is that you may not get the double-digit yields on your money you would normally get over ten years or more. A stock fund normally needs five or ten years to average out its good and bad cycles.

Leasing a Car

Question: I've been considering the purchase of a new car and have heard about the benefits of leasing. Does it ever make sense to lease instead of buy an automobile?

Answer: Yes, but only in a very few cases would I recommend that an individual lease instead of buy a car. For most people, leasing is simply a way to get into an automobile that they normally could not afford.

Let's say that you could afford only an $18,000 automobile. Through leasing you might be able to afford as much as a $25,000 automobile for the very same monthly payment and with the very same down payment, which is usually equal to the first and last month's lease payment. The problem is that you will not be building any equity in the automobile. At the end of the term, whether it's three, four or five years, you'll simply be in a position to hand the keys back. Or you could sign up for an automobile loan to pay off what's called the residual value on the note and own the car. Of course, if your income is high, you can start over again with a new car and a new, more expensive lease.

If you do decide to buy an automobile after leasing it for

five years, you would probably still owe about 35 percent of what the automobile originally sold for. So then you'd need to go and get that amount financed and probably have another two-year loan. So leasing an automobile, in my opinion, is the equivalent of financing it for about seven years, which I think is entirely too long. You will waste hundreds of dollars in interest. Most automobiles should not be financed for any longer than three to four years.

One exception to this would be people who are in business. For them there are certain tax benefits. Another exception would be some professionals who need to stay in a new car for the sake of appearance to their clients and whose time is so highly compensated that they can actually profit from buying an expensive, full-service maintenance contract (including vehicle pickup and replacement) available from some auto leasing companies.

Another consideration is small businesses that are under-capitalized. They would be able to retain some of their cash by using a lease plan. If, and only if, the money could be invested elsewhere in the business for a higher rate of return to the individual, then I would recommend using a lease.

In general, though, if these circumstances do not apply to you, a lease is simply a glamorous way of leveraging yourself.

FOUR

THE LAND MINE OF FAILING TO PLAN

A wise man thinks ahead;
a fool doesn't, and even brags about it.
Proverbs 13:16 (TLB)

The U.S. Social Security Administration says that 85 percent of Americans retire in poverty — with few assets and dependent on family, charities and Social Security for income. Many people don't make this discovery until they retire and are astonished to find themselves living at or below the poverty line.

This should be no surprise. The adage "Failing to plan is planning to fail" should be taken to heart.

Proverbs 6:6-9 says that even the ants prepare for the future. Christians have a responsibility to plan ahead. We have many issues with which to deal, including retirement, our children's education and funding charitable and religious organizations. God can use us, but only if we have enough foresight to plan.

Most people fail to plan because they are forever waiting

at the dock for their ship to come in. "When I get a raise, I will start saving," they say, or "When I get a better job, I will make sure I save some of my income," or "When my student loans are paid off, then I'll start a retirement plan." If this is your strategy, you will probably never get a savings plan started. Remember the simple ant, who doesn't make excuses.

Once you have disciplined yourself so that you are not spending more than you earn, you need to take a closer look at what you do with those earnings. As impossible as it may seem now, you can begin to save. In fact, for your own good and that of your children, you must save.

Goals

The basics of a savings plan start with setting goals. What is a goal? Some have called it a dream with a date for achievement. We must look at our circumstances and decide what we want to accomplish in the near future and the extended future.

Once we have decided on our dream, the next step is to place it on a timeline. Some people set New Year's resolutions, for example, but so many of these resolutions fail because they are not accompanied by a proper plan. A plan starts by setting a goal, establishing a deadline and then planning strategies to meet that goal within that time constraint.

For many years my family vacationed in Florida. We had a twenty-four-hour drive from Chicago. My father always had a route mapped out, and he could estimate when we would arrive. We never ended up in California or Montana — always in Florida. Why? Because my father had a plan.

Did you know that Americans spend more time planning family vacations than they do planning personal finances?

Sad, but true. We need to have a plan for our finances just as we do for other areas of life.

When I conduct seminars, invariably at least one person will approach me during a break and say, "Jim, some day I would like to be rich." I ask him for his definition of rich, and the response is usually, "I don't know — I've never really thought about it."

Someone with a goal but no plan for reaching it is setting himself up for disappointment. There is nothing very technical or magical about reaching your financial goals as long as you have a carefully conceived plan.

The components for a financial plan are:
• The desired amount of savings.
• The length of time you have to save.
• The interest rate you expect to earn (an average rate over the life of the plan).

Knowing this information will enable you to arrive at an amount you need to set aside monthly to reach that desired savings.

The easiest way to determine the components to achieve your financial goals is to obtain a financial calculator. This is like a regular pocket calculator, except it has some extra keys. It gives you the ability to compute things that would otherwise be complex to figure out. For example, you can determine what the future value will be of your savings today, based on certain interest rates. It can work out monthly payments that are necessary to meet your financial goals.

These calculators can be purchased in many stores for $20 to $30. If you have a personal computer, you may be interested in financial software that will perform these functions and much more. Such programs are available at most computer retailers. They cost between $50 and $250, depending on how sophisticated the software is. You may also want to consider special software offered through

Financial Boot Camp. The software provides a financial calculator as one of its functions, and it will be invaluable in taking control of your future. For more information, call (800) 877-2022.

The instructions included with a financial calculator will guide you through its simple operation. These keys will be of greatest value:

FV	Future Value
PV	Present Value
I	Interest Rate
PMT	Payment
N	Time

For an example, let's assume a father wants to send his newborn child to a four-year public university in eighteen years. He estimates what the tuition will be in eighteen years, and with the calculator he determines that he must save $75 per month in order to have the cash available for that school.

Saving for retirement is no different. Suppose a twenty-five-year-old woman would like to retire at age sixty-five with $1 million. She assumes that she will make an average return of 12 percent on her savings. She will need to save $85 per month for forty years in order to have $1 million upon retirement.

We can be very motivated by goals. Knowing that the $85 will lead to $1 million can put the spark in some people to make a determined effort to stick to this plan.

Goals can take many forms. Perhaps your family wishes to buy a boat. Decide how much that boat will cost and when you would like to buy it. From that data you will be able to determine how much money you will need to save monthly.

If you are planning to purchase an item for which it will

take you several years to save, keep in mind that inflation will change the price of your purchase. Base your plan on a cost that allows for a reasonable rate of inflation.

Example: Planning for Retirement

Paul and Mary Brown would like to have $500,000 for retirement when Paul is sixty-five. Paul is currently thirty-five. They assume they will be earning 8 percent interest on their investments. What is the monthly savings they need to reach their goal?

PV (present value)	=	0
FV (future value)	=	$500,000
N (time)	=	360 months (30 years)
I (interest rate)	=	8%
PMT (payment)	=	$335.48

It is very difficult to take any meaningful action on a regular basis without having a goal in mind. Do you think this couple would have the diligence to save $335.48 per month if they had no idea how much it would be worth in thirty years? Probably not.

If Paul and Mary waited until age forty to start this plan, with the same goal of $500,000 at age sixty-five, their monthly savings would need to be almost $200 more — $525. By waiting until Paul was forty-five, the monthly payment rises to $848 to accomplish the same result. At age fifty the monthly payment is a staggering $1,444!

The reason for these seemingly disproportionate increases is compound interest. The earlier savings have more years to accumulate interest, and these additional funds become part of the investment. The moral: Start saving for retirement in your early years, even if the amount is small.

You can see this principle in the work sheet in table 2 on page 63. First, determine the lump sum of money you will need upon retirement (in 1992 dollars). Your yearly income will come from the interest returns on this lump sum. For example, you may expect an interest rate of 10 percent, and you would like to have $50,000 a year when you retire. Therefore you need to accumulate a lump sum of fifty thousand times ten, or $500,000. (If you would like to calculate from a more conservative estimate of an 8 percent return, simply use a multiplier of 12 instead of 10.)

Then look at the chart in your work sheet and use your age and your expected rate of return on investing your retirement savings to find your "monthly savings cost per thousand."

Example: Buying a Car

Mike Keaton wants to pay cash for his next car. He wants to buy this automobile four years from today, when he estimates it will cost $20,000. Mike assumes that he can make 12 percent on his investment. How much will Mike need to save per month?

PV	=	0
FV	=	$20,000
N	=	48 months
I	=	12%
PMT	=	$326 per month

If Mike knows he doesn't have $326 a month to stash away, he needs to refigure. He should settle for a less expensive car or try to save for a longer period. He could assume a higher rate of return on his investment, but that would be rolling the dice.

Table 2
Retirement Funding Work Sheet

How to Decide on a Monthly Savings Plan for Retirement

Your Age Now in Years	Monthly Savings Cost Per Thousand (B) at 10% Rate of Return*	Monthly Savings Cost Per Thousand (B) at 12% Rate of Return*	Amount Needed to Equal 1,000 1992 Dollars at Time of Retirement (4% Inflation Assumed)
25	$ .78	$ .42	$4,939
30	1.07	.63	4,045
35	1.47	.95	3,313
40	2.04	1.44	2,713
45	2.93	2.25	2,222
50	4.39	3.64	1,820
55	7.27	6.48	1,490
60	15.78	14.96	1,222

1) Estimate the lump sum needed at retirement, using 1992 dollars.
_____(dollars needed per year) x 10 = _____(A)

2) Determine your monthly savings cost per thousand by referring on the above chart to your age and the expected rate of return for the money you are saving toward retirement. _____(B)

3) Use the following formula to determine monthly savings needed:

_____(A) ÷ 1,000 = _____(C)
_____(C) x _____(B) = _____(monthly savings needed)

Example: You are forty years old. Your desired income at retirement is $50,000 per year. You will invest your retirement savings in IRAs and mutual fund annuities and hope to realize a rate of return at an average of 12 percent. How much do you need to save per month to realize your goal?

$50,000 (income per year) x 10 = $500,000 (A)
$500,000 (A) ÷ 1,000 = 500 (C)
500 (C) x $1.44 (B) = $720 (monthly savings needed)

*After-tax rates of return are used because most money should be in qualified retirement plans, IRAs and mutual fund annuities, which are not taxed until after retirement. Assumed retirement age is sixty-five years.

Example: Saving for College

Anita and Bill Thompson have a five-year-old daughter, Amanda. They wish to send her to college at age eighteen. They plan to have $50,000 for this purpose. Bill feels that 10 percent is a reasonable rate of return. How much should they set aside?

PV	=	0
FV	=	$50,000
N	=	156 months (13 years)
I	=	10%
PMT	=	$157 per month

College costs are rising 7 to 9 percent per year, which is steeper than the rate of inflation. Bill and Anita should watch college costs and inflation closely in case they need to adjust their goal and, consequently, their savings.

Example: Mired in Debt

Tina Reynolds bought a car last year and also got a little loose with her credit cards at Christmas. Now she owes $20,000 in consumer debt. The average of all the interest rates she is currently paying is 15 percent. She wants to be out of debt in two years. How much will she need to pay each month to reach her goal?

PV	=	$20,000
FV	=	0
N	=	24 months
I	=	15%
PMT	=	$969 per month

She should pay off the credit cards with the highest interest rates first in order to bring down the high cost of the interest she is paying. And, of course, cutting up those cards so as not to incur more debt is essential!

Example: Paying Off Mortgage Early

Mike and Connie Hall have a thirty-year mortgage at 8 percent fixed interest. They are interested in prepaying the principal balance in order to own the house free and clear in ten years. The mortgage amount is $100,000; and their current payment is $733 per month.

What should they be paying in order to retire the mortgage in ten years?

PV	=	$100,000
FV	=	0
N	=	120 months
I	=	8%
PMT	=	$1,213 per month (additional principal payments of $480)

The interest rates in these examples are simply for illustration. You should be aware of the current trends in interest rates in order to make sound estimates for your planning. I will discuss interest rates later in the context of properly investing your money.

Summary

Setting goals is critical to financial success. In order to reach these goals, you must first quantify them. How much? How soon? What are your dreams? How much would you like to have set aside for retirement? Put your goals in writing, with careful attention to the specifics.

Second, the goals must be accompanied by a plan that

includes a time frame. Having no plan for your financial future means that you are allowing precious months and years to slip away. This is the most dangerous land mine of all because it is a slow killer; but it cannot be reversed. Time can be your greatest ally or your greatest enemy. Once you realize that you have neglected to plan, it may be too late.

Stick with the plan. Set aside those payments. Monitor the plan every six months by checking the rate of inflation and the interest rates that you are earning to decide if you need to modify your plan.

Even if you have to start out on a small scale, such as saving $10 each month, the important thing is that you have grasped the concept and have caught the vision to plan for the future. Getting started is the first hurdle; continuing to save is essential to the result.

Are financial goals a priority in your life? Are they important enough to warrant some of your attention? I think they are, and I urge you to spend time developing those goals and the plans to make them work.

Questions

Planning With Variable Income

Question: Because I am self-employed, I'm not quite sure what amount of money I am going to make from month to month. It varies so much that it's difficult for me to follow the principles you teach about setting up a plan.

Answer: Situations such as this are becoming more common as people start their own businesses and become more entrepreneurial. If you are self-employed or perhaps in sales, where your income fluctuates, you need to see what your average earnings are.

Let's say in a six-month period your income is $2,000 the first month, $2,000 the second month, $0 the third month, $6,000 the fourth month, $0 the fifth month and $2,000 in the sixth month.

Your total income is $12,000, or $2,000 per month. So base your budget and your investment plan on the $2,000 per month average income. The temptation is to spend everything you make each month, but this is dangerous because you are not compensating for the months where you earn nothing.

FIVE

The Land Mine
of Insufficient
College Funding

How much better to get wisdom than gold.
Proverbs 16:16

As Christians we want some basic things for our children: that they would know Jesus Christ as their Savior when they are young and that they would exhibit Christian character as they grow up. But beyond those foundational matters, we would all like to see our children prepare themselves adequately for a fulfilling career.

If our children are to be able to compete in the 1990s and beyond, they are going to need a solid educational foundation. For some that will mean a traditional college education; for others it will mean specialized vocational training. I believe that in the next ten years post-secondary education is going to change radically.

For example, my wife, who is a school teacher, told me she had to take two night classes to update her teaching certification. So when I came home from work on the day of her class I was surprised to find her sitting on the couch watching television. I wondered if she had forgotten to go to school, but I discovered she was taking one of her classes through a local-access cable channel.

While this shows how educational formats are becoming more nontraditional, and perhaps may be available at reduced costs, all indications are that parents should expect hefty bills for their children's college educations. That means more planning.

Escalating Costs

In 1992 the CBS television affiliate in Orlando asked me to do a report on college educational costs. I compared today's costs with projected costs for a newborn, who would be going to college in eighteen years. I contacted experts across the country who have been tracking these costs for the last twenty years. Amazingly, the cost of a college education has been increasing at an annual rate of 7 to 8 percent. That's almost twice the current rate of inflation!

I called some major universities and asked for their tuition rates. Then I used a financial calculator to determine how much a four-year education would cost in eighteen to twenty-four years, using an 8 percent rate of inflation. Here are the results, for tuition only for the year 2010:

Harvard University	$208,000
Notre Dame University	176,000
Florida State University*	16,900
University of Central Florida*	17,700

Using the financial calculator further, I checked to see what parents would need to save on a monthly basis in order to send their newborn to college in eighteen years. I assumed a 12 percent rate of interest. Here are the results:

Harvard University	$274.00
Notre Dame University	232.00
Florida State University*	23.00
University of Central Florida*	23.50

*In-state tuition

You can research the college of your choice and plug the numbers into a financial calculator to find out the same costs.

One difficult part of the planning is trying to determine what kind of post-secondary education each child will need. Our children are unique. Just because Dad is a doctor doesn't necessarily mean that little Johnny is interested in becoming a doctor. We must listen to each child to discover his or her interests — perhaps it will be music or art; maybe the mechanics of an engine fascinate him. It is very destructive to try to put your child into a career for which he does not have a passion.

At the same time we want to be able to provide our children with an education that will give them a foothold in the real world. They should be prepared to make a living for themselves in a world where many of the job descriptions of the future do not even exist now, just as today's computer-related jobs did not exist twenty-five years ago. Whatever path they may end up taking, we know one thing is certain: Our decision to save for their education or vocational training cannot be put off until the last minute.

A caller to my national radio show asked me how she could best save for her son's college education. Before I gave her my recommendations on investments, I asked how old her son was. "He's seventeen," she said. Unfortunately this woman had waited too long.

The key to funding a college education is starting to save when the child is young. As I've said before, time can be your greatest ally or your worst enemy when it comes to saving money. I believe in using time to your greatest advantage.

For example, you must save $274 per month when the child is born to be ready to write checks to Harvard University. If you wait until that child is ten years old, the monthly payment balloons to $1,300 per month. In the case of the Florida State University education, if you waited ten years before saving, the schedule would be $105 per month, more than four times the amount you would be setting aside if you had started saving earlier. The college savings guide in table 3 on page 73 shows how critical it is to begin a college savings program when your child is young so that you can keep your monthly payments at a minimum.

Once you have estimated the total cost for the four years of college, you can take your child's age and compute how much you need to save monthly, expecting a 10 percent or 12 percent rate of return, to have the college payment ready by high school graduation (see table 4 on page 74).

Don't Be Shy With College Funds

In order for your child to have a traditional college education, especially at a private school, you will have to be a nontraditional investor. Let me explain. Most people, whether they are parents or well-meaning relatives, tend to be overconservative when they invest on behalf of a child's education. Many of the most popular investments for this purpose include Series EE U.S. savings bonds, certificates of deposit, savings accounts and other government securities.

These investments historically have not kept pace with college education costs, which are increasing 7 percent to 8 percent per year. So your money will not be working hard enough for your children.

You need to earn at least 8 percent on your college nest egg. It would be better still to earn *more* than the rate at which college tuition is rising. A good choice would be to look for investments earning 12 percent on the average, over ten or twenty years.

When most people look at the stock market, their initial reaction is fear. We all have vivid memories of October 1987, when the market crashed. Events such as this have given the stock market a bad reputation regarding risk, specifically over long periods of time. The stock market, over a long period of time, presents a low-risk, high-return opportunity. While it is true that the stock market has its downward spirals for months and occasionally for years, the long-term investor in the stock market has made money. Stock appreciation has far exceeded the inflation rate over decades.

When funding a college education, look for a mutual fund, such as those listed in appendices F and G. The fund should have a good track record over ten years or more and should be doing well currently. For more information on long-term investing, see the chapter on the land mine of bad investments.

My goal in this chapter is to persuade you to be a non-traditional investor for your children's college and career education funding. I know it can be scary to place that money in the stock market and then pick up the newspaper and watch the price of your mutual fund going up one day and down the next. But if you will look at the fund's long-term record, I'm sure you will be confident that investing in the market and avoiding the low-return government securities and bank CDs is the right choice.

Table 3
College Funding Guide

Monthly Savings Required (in 1992 Dollars) for Each $1,000 of College Tuition Needed

- 10% Interest on Savings
- 12% Interest on Savings

Age of Children

Age	10% Interest on Savings	12% Interest on Savings
Newborn	$7.00	$5.54
3 Years	$7.98	$6.62
8 Years	$9.42	$8.16
10 Years	$10.83	$9.65
13 Years	$19.22	$18.23
15 Years	$30.40	$29.48

Table 4
College Funding Work Sheet

How to Decide on a Monthly Savings Plan for Your Child's College Tuition

Child's Age Now in Years	Monthly Savings Cost Per Thousand (B) at 10% Rate of Return*	Monthly Savings Cost Per Thousand (B) at 12% Rate of Return*	Amount Needed to Equal 1,000 1992 Dollars at Time of High School Graduation (8% Inflation Assumed)
Newborn	$ 7.00	$ 5.54	$4,200
3	7.98	6.62	3,306
8	9.42	8.16	2,603
10	10.83	9.65	2,219
13	19.22	18.23	1,489
15	30.40	29.48	1,270

1) Estimate the total cost of a college education for your child, using 1992 dollars. _____(A)

2) Determine your monthly savings cost per thousand by referring on the above chart to the age of your child and the expected rate of return for the money you are saving toward college tuition. _____(B)

3) Use the following formula to determine monthly savings needed.

_____(A) + 1,000 = _____(C)
_____(C) x _____(B) = _____(monthly savings needed)

Example: Your child is three years old. You estimate that it will cost $20,000 to put him/her through college. You will invest money toward his/her education and hope to realize a rate of return at an average of 12 percent. How much do you need to save per month to realize your goal?

$20,000 (A) ÷ 1,000 = 20 (C)
20 (C) x $6.62 (B) = $132.40 (monthly savings needed)

*After-tax rates of return are used because a mutual fund annuity, which is not taxed until the money is withdrawn, should be used for this investment.

Financial Aid

For those of you reading this chapter whose children are in grade school or even high school, your choices are admittedly diminished. Many people have asked me if they should take a second mortgage on their home or take out a student loan from the government. Normally I discourage such steps until all other resources have been exhausted.

The first consideration should be consulting with the financial aid office at the college or technical school your child wishes to attend. Perhaps there are scholarships available. Many corporations and private individuals offer scholarships to students of all interests.

You should start looking for grants and scholarships long before your child is ready to pack his or her belongings into the family van. By the child's sixteenth birthday, start looking into funding sources. One of the experts on college funding is Daniel J. Cassidy, the president of National Scholarship Research Service [2280 Airport Boulevard, Santa Rosa, CA 95403; (707) 546-6777]. His service sells a variety of reference materials, many of them available in libraries. For a fee the firm will search data bases nationwide to come up with a computer printout of scholarships, loans and programs that will fit your circumstance.

As a guest on my radio show, Cassidy reiterated that a student need not be a tremendous athlete or scholar to qualify for the myriad of scholarship monies available. The David Letterman Scholarship, for example, is made available to students going to Ball State University in Indiana who have a low grade-point average! Cassidy knew of another scholarship where the student must have a particular last name to qualify.

Remember to start your scholarship search early. Most of the monies are allocated by the middle of the student's senior year.

Beware of student loans. I recall a talk show examining "deadbeat doctors" — doctors who went to medical school on student loans and then refused to pay them back or were slow in paying their loans. Part of the problem is that a young doctor is usually overwhelmed with thousands of dollars of debt from his prolonged, expensive schooling. It often takes ten years or longer to repay this debt.

Loans for school may be easy to obtain, but they are very difficult to repay. It is a great burden to a young person just getting started in a career to be saddled with debt that takes years to repay. I know people whose parents promised to pay back the loans and then were unable or unwilling to do so, leaving a twenty-three-year-old with thousands of dollars of debt.

I recommend financing schooling without borrowed money if at all possible. Even if it means that the student is in school for six to eight years as he works his way through, this is far preferable to borrowing.

I recommend to undergraduates who are planning graduate work to take a year or two off and work, saving for their education and getting some solid work experience for their resumés.

Summary

Make time work for you, not against you, by starting a college savings plan as early as possible. Use mutual funds for the best possible returns.

If you have waited too late to be able to set up an adequate savings plan, get help in researching scholarships and encourage your child to work while in school. Avoid student loans if at all possible.

For further materials regarding college and occupational choices, consult appendix D.

SIX

THE LAND MINE OF INSUFFICIENT RETIREMENT FUNDING

If a person lives to be very old,
let him rejoice in every day of life.
Ecclesiastes 11:8 (TLB)

Most working Americans have a great opportunity at their fingertips, but they let it pass by them every day. I'm talking about failure to participate in a corporate retirement plan.

In her book *Social Insecurity*, Dorcas Hardy, former commissioner of the Social Security administration, points out that by 2010 there will be serious financial problems with Social Security benefits because the proportion of workers to retirees will be much lower than in previous years. Though I am not trying to predict the future of our economic system or of the Social Security system, as others have, it is unwise to put great faith in receiving benefits from this system when you reach retirement.

Additionally, Social Security was never intended to be your sole means of financial support upon retirement. It was intended simply to *supplement* your retirement plan. Therefore, you should make other arrangements.

Once I was a guest on a Washington, D.C., radio talk show developed mainly to help answer the needs of government employees. The issue this day was one of the government retirement plans designed for U.S. Postal Service employees. Prior to the program I found that this retirement plan was providing a match of nearly 50 percent. In other words, for every dollar that the employee contributed, the government would kick in 50 cents. Even if the money never earned a penny of interest, the employee was already realizing a 50 percent return. Not bad!

This is not an unusual plan nor an unusual level of matching. People across the country have corporate retirement plans that do the same thing. They can take pre-tax dollars and invest them in government bonds, corporate bonds, stock funds or a money market account. According to my research, only about 50 percent of the employees of corporations offering these types of programs are taking advantage of them.

The retirement funding work sheet in chapter 4 helped you determine the lump sum of money you would need at retirement. You could also calculate the monthly payments you would need to make to accumulate that amount, taking into account growth from interest. But think how much faster your money would grow if a certain percentage of your investment were matched by your company as well.

You do not have to be a highly paid executive to build a significant nest egg. I have talked with school teachers who have built up $150,000 or $200,000 in their plan upon retirement, and they come to me for further information on how to invest this money.

A newspaper article told about a U.S. Postal Service employee who had utilized this plan for more than forty years. He started by putting $5 of his $32 paycheck into the plan each week. Eventually the employee established an $800,000 scholarship fund at Louisiana Tech University. The university expects a 7.5 percent return on this investment, and they expect it to grow to more than $1 million, providing more than $56,000 per year in scholarship funds.

If this is what a postal worker can do for a university, what could Christians do for the Lord's kingdom simply by following the basic principle of saving for the future?

Corporate retirement plans, such as a 401(k) or a 403(b), are an excellent way of saving for your future for three reasons. First, the money is normally taken right out of your paycheck so that you never miss the funds because they are never available for you to spend. Second, the plans usually use pre-tax dollars, and the interest grows tax-deferred, which means you don't pay income taxes on the money until it is removed from the plan. (For more information, see chapter 14 on the land mine of poor tax planning.) Third, many corporations offer matches of 10 percent, 20 percent or even 50 percent as an incentive for employees to use the fund.

Proverbs 21:5 (TLB) says, "Steady plodding brings prosperity; hasty speculation brings poverty." The corporate retirement plan, like any other methodical savings program, is a prime example of steady plodding.

Deciding to place savings in a matching retirement plan usually leads to another decision: Where do you invest that money? Most such plans offer a small number of choices to the employee. Over long periods, the best choice historically has been the stock market. If you are given the choice between a money market fund, bond funds or stock fund, I would recommend a well-diversified stock fund.

Many people, through loyalty, are attracted to purchasing stock in the corporation they work for. My only caution on buying company stock is that you are placing all of your money in one place. Should something adverse happen to your company, your funds could be in jeopardy. If they had been placed in a diversified stock fund, there would be less chance of taking a substantial loss. If your corporate stock appeals to you, my recommendation is to split up your retirement funds, if possible, and place no more than 10 percent in your employer's stock. Put the rest in a diversified stock mutual fund.

In the chapter on mutual funds I will discuss market timing and moving your money into and out of stocks and bonds, based on market climate. Unfortunately it is rather cumbersome to do this with funds in a corporate retirement plan. The reason is that the corporation normally limits how often per year you can move your money. Some plans allow only once a year; others will allow a move once a quarter. I recommend the buy-and-hold strategy because of the lack of flexibility. Pick a good mutual fund or two, and possibly some company stock, and keep the funds in place unless you see a dramatic change in the market.

When the Money Passes to You

Understand that you may end up with this money before you retire. The money will be distributed if you are terminated, if you resign or if the plan is discontinued. If you die, it will go to your spouse or other beneficiary. The money becomes immediately taxable unless it is "rolled over" (converted) into an individual retirement account (IRA) within sixty days. Normally you can place only $2,000 per year in your IRA, but in the case of a retirement account distribution under the circumstances just mentioned, the entire amount can be placed in your IRA without any tax penalty.

For example, I handled a large estate for a woman whose husband died in an auto accident. The IRS allowed the surviving spouse to roll those retirement funds into her personal retirement account. This rule does not apply to surviving children or other relatives but only to the surviving spouse.

When an individual retires, the company may recommend that the retiree take a monthly payment option for the rest of his or her life. I have found that this is not the best way to receive your retirement plan. I recommend that you take a lump sum distribution and roll those funds into an IRA from one of the major mutual fund companies.

Next, I recommend that you structure a monthly distribution to yourself of 8 percent annualized. Let me give you an example. You receive $500,000 upon your retirement. You roll this entire amount into an IRA with Fidelity, a mutual fund family. You then purchase five mutual funds of $100,000 each within that IRA, and each year you remove 8 percent of the monies from each of the funds. (You can split this up into monthly payments.) This gives you $40,000 each year, or $3,333 per month. At the end of the year you will have to pay taxes on that $40,000 income.

On April 15 of the following year, take monies from your IRA to pay the taxes.

Remember that mutual funds move up and down with the market climate. Buy good mutual funds and hold them, with occasional moves, if necessary, as the market indicates. Don't panic. Your funds are paying full-time professionals to watch the market and anticipate the kinds of changes that provoke unstable investors to make foolish decisions.

By following this strategy over a long period of time, my clients have had outstanding results. They have been able to receive more than double the benefit offered by an employer by taking the lump sum and investing it as I have recommended. Even if that fixed payment option includes a partial benefit to the surviving spouse upon your death, the fixed payment plan still does not meet with the same good results as the lump sum plan.

Of course, you aren't required to take 8 percent per year out of the plan. Perhaps you wish to leave the money in the IRA mutual funds for several years, allowing the money to build up more interest, and then you will start taking monies out at 8 percent, or even a smaller rate. I use the 8 percent annualized amount as an example, to compare it to what would normally be a lower monthly payment in the option offered by corporations, which also leaves little or nothing to your survivors when you die.

If you feel uncomfortable managing your own retirement distribution, there are organizations that can provide this service for a nominal annual fee. They will place your money in mutual funds and provide a tracking service, while at the same time distributing the monies to you on a monthly basis. Ask a Christian friend for a referral of financial planners in your community. [If you don't know anyone to ask, you may call James L. Paris Financial Services at (800) 950-PLAN.]

Summary

I hope I have persuaded you to take advantage of your employer's retirement plan. Some are better than others, but all are better than no retirement plan at all. Consider the wisdom of Proverbs 10:5: "He who gathers crops in summer is a wise son, but he who sleeps during harvest is a disgraceful son."

I challenge you to forego the protest that you need every penny from your weekly paycheck and that you can't afford to use the retirement plan. Proverbs 21:20 (TLB) says, "The wise man saves for the future, but the foolish man spends whatever he gets." If you are in debt, make a plan to get out of debt, but don't neglect to save for your retirement. We must, as good stewards of the Lord's money, save something for our older years, and even $1 per week invested in a corporate retirement account, even without matching funds, is $1 invested wisely for the future. If you don't use your retirement plan, you are only hurting yourself and your family.

Questions

What Return to Expect

Question: When you talk about goal setting, I hear you use numbers such as 10 percent or 12 percent. I don't necessarily think that I can earn those rates of return on my money. Should I still set goals on that basis even though those rates of return may not be applicable to me?

Answer: People often ask me this in my seminars. Since they may not have had the experience of making double-digit returns, they are rightfully skeptical. But, remember, the concept is simple. Don't let me or anyone else decide what your goals should be, what the rate of return on your money will be or the length of time that you will be saving. Those are all personal decisions.

Decide what you want and quantify how much money it will take to get you there, whether it is a retirement plan, funding your children's education, buying a new home, a new car and so on. Determine how long you have to save the money, what assumed interest rate you are going to make and how long it is going to take for you to accomplish that. Set up a plan to make a monthly deposit into a mutual fund account. If you stick to that plan, you should reach your goal. Following these guidelines, I have found that a 10 or 12 percent return over long terms is not unreasonable.

Savings Versus Retiring Debt

Question: Some people say I should pay off all of my

debt before I start investing. I'm really excited about your mutual fund concepts and would like to start investing, but I do have debt. How do I decide how much money I should put toward debt reduction and how much I should invest?

Answer: I believe that the main reason some people have a large amount of debt is that they never established a commitment to savings. Because they never had a financial reserve, they had no option but to use credit cards every time they got into a bind.

Those who handle their finances this way will never be out of debt. They're not learning the discipline of putting away money on a monthly basis so they can draw from it when an emergency occurs instead of borrowing money. So I recommend channeling 50 percent of the surplus funds to debt repayment and 50 percent to investment.

I believe that most often the truth can be found between the extremes. It is extreme to say that a person should pay off all of their debt before investing. Also, it is an extreme to say that people should not worry about paying off their debt and simply invest the money.

Government Bonds

Question: Are government bonds always a safe way to invest?

Answer: Most people are ignorant of how interest rate volatility can greatly affect the value of bonds, even government bonds. This was especially true in the early 1980s, as interest rates skyrocketed.

For every 1 percent increase in the prime rate, the average bond portfolio loses about 10 percent of its value. That meant that in 1979 and 1980, with rapidly rising interest rates, government bond investors could have lost more than 30 to 40 percent of their principal.

How can that happen? you ask. Aren't government bonds guaranteed by the government? Yes, they are. What is guaranteed by the government is the timely payment of interest and principal upon maturity. But there is more going on here.

Managers of a government bond fund most likely will not hold the bonds until maturity. They will always be buying and selling the bonds to keep the best yields possible in the portfolio. What that means is that when the market value of the bond goes down because of interest rate increases, the value of that bond mutual fund goes down. Remember, when interest rates go up, bonds and bond funds go down. This includes corporate and government bonds.

As I mentioned earlier, for a 1 percent increase in the prime rate, most bonds will drop about 10 percent or more. Of course, the reverse is also true. Many people have made a great deal of money in bonds by buying them when interest rates are dropping. When interest rates are dropping, for every 1 percent drop in the prime rate, expect an approximate gain of 10 percent or more in the average bond and bond portfolio.

Withheld Pension Benefits

Question: My company refuses to release the amount of pension benefits I am entitled to, even though I resigned over two years ago. What are my rights?

Answer: File a complaint with the U.S. Department of Labor, Pension and Welfare Benefits Administration [(202) 523-8776]. Additionally, I would recommend filing a complaint with the Internal Revenue Service, which would be very interested in any improper usage of pension funds. Even the threat of filing this kind of complaint can be all you need to get fair treatment.

SEVEN

THE LAND MINE
OF BAD
INVESTMENTS

Dishonest money dwindles away,
but he who gathers money little by little makes it grow.
Proverbs 13:11

You may be familiar with Matthew 25:14-30, where Jesus tells the parable of a master who goes on a long journey and leaves some money, or "talents," with each of his three servants. The word *talent* comes from the Greek *talanton*, meaning "a coin or a sum of money." One servant receives five units of money, another receives two units, and the last receives one unit.

After the master returns, he requires an accounting. The first two servants doubled their money through wise investment, and the master praises and rewards them. The servant who had been given one talent gives the master back the one talent, explaining that he had done nothing with it because he was afraid. Because he did not try to invest his master's money for its best use, this servant is severely punished for his inaction and his attitude.

86

This passage should compel us to make the most of what the Lord gives. That's one reason I am concerned when I see Christians making bad investments.

In this chapter I will review what I consider to be some of the best and worst investments in America. I have been able to study more than five thousand clients' investment portfolios, which include a wide variety of investments. Therefore, I have seen firsthand which investments work and which should be avoided.

A good rule of thumb is that *the more exotic the investment, the poorer the results were for the investor.* For some reason — often greed, because of the chance for a fast, large return — some of us are drawn to unusual types of investments. We may find ourselves in very speculative ventures, hoping for the big payoff, which usually never materializes. In making such choices, we shun the tried and true paths of wise investing.

Here are, in my opinion, America's five worst investment land mines:

• *Time-share Units*

This is the very worst "investment" of the five. I live in Florida, a hotbed for time-shares. A time-share, also called an interval ownership unit, initially was a good concept. If you could not afford to buy a summer or vacation home, you could buy one or two weeks' use of a resort. These weeks were theoretically exchangeable with weeks at other time-share resorts across the country. Therefore, if you owned a week at a ski resort in Colorado, you should have been able to trade your week with someone who may have owned a week at a resort in Daytona Beach, Florida.

The problems with these units are that they are extremely overpriced, they involve maintenance fees that can increase rapidly, and they are usually difficult to sell for the price you paid for them. For my research, I have visited some of these time-shares and have noted that the marketing technique is very aggressive. In many states laws have been passed to regulate their marketing. In Florida salespeople are forbidden to call time-shares "investments" because the term is misleading. Time-shares are clearly *not* an investment.

Time-share salespeople will compare the time-share to single-family real estate, which traditionally has enjoyed good appreciation. Just as your home increases in value, they say, so will the time-share. This is simply untrue. When I did a report on time-share units for the local CBS television affiliate in Orlando, I uncovered some startling facts. Time-share units can be purchased on the resale secondary market for about 40 percent of their original price. This means that if you buy a time-share directly from the developer, you can count on losing 60 percent of your investment the minute you sign the contract. Does that sound like a good deal?

If you are seriously considering buying a time-share, look in the classified ads for a used time-share, because the bargains are there for the picking. I have nothing against buying a time-share for the use and enjoyment of it, just as you would purchase a health club membership. But don't consider it an investment — because it's not.

• *Penny Stocks*

Penny stocks are considered to be those that sell for less than $5 per share. These stocks are quite risky. Unscrupulous stockbrokers sell them with promises of huge returns. After all, if a stock bought at $1 rises to $3, you have tripled your money. These stocks are also sold over the telephone — and I warn you never to purchase stock at any price from an unsolicited telephone sales call! I can tell you story after story of people who have purchased penny stocks with their life savings, only to have the company disappear, along with their money.

The Securities and Exchange Commission (SEC) and the

National Association of Securities Dealers (NASD) have implemented some strict disclosures that are required by those selling penny stocks. They must have you sign a disclaimer, saying that you are aware of the risk involved. This should be a red flag to anyone buying these stocks.

Most people who are attracted to high-risk penny stocks are looking for rapid riches. I've observed that people who run after get-rich-quick schemes get poor quick.

In this list of speculative investing, I would also include options and futures contracts on stocks or commodities, such as pork bellies or soybeans. These investments amount to betting a price will go up or down a specified amount over a certain period — not something for the unseasoned investor.

• *Rare Coins*

The market for coins has become more regulated, thus improving the value of the investment in coins. Many major brokerage firms are getting involved in selling coins.

However, I am still not convinced that this is a good investment for most people. My clients who have invested in coins have been very dissatisfied. When they try to sell the coins, they are worth less than the original sales price. The main reason for this is dealer markup. When you buy a coin for $1,000, chances are that the dealer paid only $600 for that same coin. He has to make a profit to stay in business, and the markup is usually 60 to 100 percent.

Let's say that two or three years from now the coin has appreciated in value by 10 percent, so now its retail value is $1,100. If you take it to a coin dealer he will offer you $675, the wholesale price for the coin. Even though your coin has appreciated, it is difficult for a collector to resell the coin at retail and make a profit. You could obtain a higher price by finding another investor or collector, but this would require yet another investment — lots of your time. And you would still probably have to take a loss.

• Collectibles

Collectibles include baseball cards, sports memorabilia, antiques, art and any number of other items people are known to collect. You'll find the same problem here with dealer markup as in the coin industry. Dealers buy collectibles at wholesale price and add a healthy markup. It is more difficult for an investor or collector to find retail buyers for this merchandise, so most people go to dealers and end up losing money. Retail baseball card shops, for example, pay customers 50 to 60 percent of the worth of the card, which is listed in Beckett's, the primary price guide. If you buy the same card at the shop, you'll pay about 100 percent of what the guide says.

Generally speaking, if you are not an expert or a dealer in these fields, avoid collectibles for investment purposes. Buy antiques or baseball cards to own them; but do not consider them investments because rarely will you make money in their resale.

You don't want to take an undue risk with money set aside for retirement or the children's education. I have seen many people lose large sums through collectibles.

• Jewelry

Jewelry is another example of what you and I can buy only at *retail* prices and usually cannot resell at any price above wholesale. A friend of mine has a diamond ring she purchased for $2,000 years ago. She recently had it appraised, and to her delight the diamond itself was worth $2,200. Out of curiosity she took it to a jeweler and offered to sell the ring. He offered her $1,600. Why? Because he planned to sell it for $2,200 and make a $600 profit.

I have heard people try to justify extravagant jewelry purchases by saying that it will be a good investment some day. This may be the case *if* that person can find a buyer who will pay the retail price.

Again, buy jewelry to wear it. Don't consider it an

investment, and don't put your life savings or your retirement account into jewelry.

Only if you are an expert in art, jewelry, antiques or other collectibles can you make money. It involves years of training and experience to acquire the degree of expertise (you should probably be a dealer!) and contacts you will need to be on top of your field. But 99.9 percent of the consumer population should stick with the investments I am about to discuss — mutual funds, stocks and bonds. These investments, boring though they sound, most likely will appreciate and are highly liquid, meaning you will have no trouble finding a buyer to pay top dollar.

Risk and Reality

While there are those too eager to assume the risk of collectibles and time-shares, the more common problem is risk phobia. Many Christians are guilty of being too conservative with their investment philosophy and are therefore not meeting their financial goals. "Nothing ventured, nothing gained" is very applicable when it comes to investing. Most risk is overstated, and, therefore, most people will overreact by being too conservative, leaving themselves in grave financial condition at retirement.

For example, many Christians fear the stock market, so they run to their local bank to invest because the Federal Deposit Insurance Corporation (FDIC), a government agency, insures their deposits up to $100,000. This is a mistake. Banks are notorious for paying low interest rates on deposits. The banking industry gives us security in the FDIC in exchange for extremely meager earnings. Most bank certificates of deposit (CDs) do not even keep up with the rate of inflation, so if you consider the buying power of your money, your investments lose money each year to inflation. This is one reason why I refer to bank CDs as "certificates of depreciation." Putting your savings into the bank is no different from being like the third servant in the parable, who buried the master's money in the ground.

To understand the importance of getting a good return, consider again the Rule of 72 that I mentioned earlier. This simple mathematical shortcut tells you how many years it will take for your investment to double at any given interest rate. If you divide the rate of return on an investment into 72, you get the number of years it will take for your money to double.

Take two individuals who have $10,000 each to invest. One earns 6 percent and the other 12 percent for twenty-four years. Then divide six into seventy-two and divide twelve into seventy-two. You learn that the money earning 6 percent will double every *twelve* years, and the money earning 12 percent will double every *six* years. The first individual has $40,000 at the end of twenty-four years, and the second has $160,000! Why the huge difference? If the rate of return was only twice as much, how could the result be four times greater? The answer is in the magic of compound interest.

Many Baskets for Your Eggs

But, you may ask, isn't the person earning 12 percent at more risk of losing all his money than the person investing in 6 percent CDs? Indeed, the risk is higher. But under a wise investing program, especially one spread over several years, it is very unlikely that the return on an investment will be as low as a bank CD, and it is virtually impossible to lose much of the principal, which is the original investment. The key to managing the risk factor is *diversification*. It is unwise to put all your money into one investment.

Consider an individual who invests a total of $10,000 in five different programs and has the following results over twenty years:

Investment	Return
$2,000	-100% (loses it all)
$2,000	0% (makes nothing, loses nothing)
$2,000	15% average return over twenty years
$2,000	12% average return over twenty years
$2,000	5% average return over twenty years

Total Return: $68,640

If this investor had purchased 7 percent CDs with his money, he would have ended up with $28,000 less! Diversification is the key. If you are afraid to take risks, you will guarantee yourself a low return. (To illustrate this further, see appendix E for the real rate of return on CDs.)

Remember that taxes and inflation will play a major part in the results of your investment. During recent years you could earn 500 percent interest in Brazil — the only problem was that Brazil's inflation rate was 1,000 percent, so you would end up losing money. In order to make a full evaluation of the return on investment, you must determine what economists call *real interest*. Real interest is the amount an investor earns after inflation. In the economy of the early 1990s, with inflation running at 4.5 percent, an investment yielding 5.5 to 6 percent is earning only 1 to 1.5 percent real interest.

I remember a news story about Congressman Dan Rostenkowski of Illinois, who proposed a temporary discontinuation of the cost of living adjustment for Social Security recipients. Retired individuals across the country protested in every way imaginable. The climax was when a group of senior citizens trapped Rostenkowski in his automobile!

Yet, ironically, these same retirees, who would not stand

for one moment to be passed by for an annual increase of benefits, are often purchasing investments that bring yields just above inflation. After paying taxes, these investments sometimes have a net negative result! It is no wonder that more than 85 percent of retirees are in need of supplemental financial assistance.

Mutual Funds

If you found that someone had developed a system for making money that was working, you would probably be attracted to it. From reviewing client portfolios over the years, I discovered not only the investments that didn't work, but also those that, in almost every case, made money.

I concluded that America's best investment, in terms of balancing risk with a good return, is the mutual fund. This is a fund in which thousands of investors pool their money in the purchase of a portfolio of corporate stocks or bonds. That portfolio, which is professionally managed, allows for diversification due to the large volume of money being pooled.

To give you an idea of how a mutual fund works, let's say that you have one thousand friends who have $100 each to invest. With $100, the individual can buy only one or two shares of most stocks. However, if you could convince those one thousand friends to pool their money, you would have $100,000 to purchase a variety of stocks, giving you broad diversification. Each investor would own a piece of that portfolio. This is basically how a mutual fund operates.

The mutual fund company makes money through management of its portfolios. Each portfolio is placed in the care of a manager, who watches the market very closely and makes adjustments, buying and selling stocks within the mutual fund, in order to make and keep the fund profitable. An investor in mutual funds pays this manager a small fee each year, usually about 1 percent of the money he invested, for the management of this fund.

Mutual funds have been around for close to eighty years. They didn't receive much attention until the early 1970s. Most stockbrokers didn't talk much about mutual funds because they would rather have you buy individual stocks, thereby generating commissions to them each time the stocks are bought and sold.

I like mutual funds for three reasons:

• *Low minimum investment*

One mutual fund company, Twentieth Century Investors, allows you to get started with as little as a $1 investment. To obtain information from Twentieth Century, call (800) 345-2021.

Although this company is a rare exception, there are many mutual funds that allow you to invest with as little as between $250 and $1,000.

If you find it difficult to save on a regular basis, you can even arrange for an automatic draft from your checking account for your monthly investment. The automatic draft saves time as well.

• *Diversification*

Mutual funds allow for a wide range of diversification with your investment. Diversification is your hedge against risk.

• *Low expenses*

Annual management fees for most mutual funds cost you no more than 1 percent of the money you have invested in the company, especially if you opt for no-load mutual funds, which require no up-front fee.

Today there are more mutual funds than there are stocks that trade on the New York Stock Exchange. There are two basic types of mutual funds in terms of their fees: loaded funds, for which a commission is paid to a salesperson when you purchase shares in the fund, and no-load funds, for which there is no fee when you purchase shares. There are more than three thousand mutual funds, but only four hundred are no-load. Of course, I prefer the no-load funds. They are just as sound as the loaded funds, but you save that up-front commission charge.

Stockbrokers and financial planners can charge you up to 9 percent of your initial investment as a commission. So if you put $1,000 into a loaded mutual fund, you will have invested as little as $910 because the other $90 went into a broker's pocket. Financial salespeople do not like no-load mutual funds because they don't make any money on them. In fact, there are three lies you may hear from these brokers. These are:

• *Loaded funds outperform no-load funds.* This is simply untrue. Commission fees have nothing to do with performance. Loaded funds simply have a commission built into the structure. The money does not go into the mutual fund, but rather to the salesperson who sells the investment.

• *Nothing is for free.* All mutual fund companies charge an annual management fee, so you still end up paying more for a loaded fund than if you buy a no-load fund of the same value.

• *No-load funds have higher expenses.* This, too, is false. No-load mutual fund companies charge the same or *less* in management fees each year, an average of 1 percent.

Finding a Fund

The three keys to choosing a mutual fund are:
• Economic climate
• Momentum
• Historical performance (track record)
Let's examine these elements.
It would be foolish to say that you always should be

investing in the stock market or always should be investing in the bond market. Economies change, and circumstances change, and investors should make adjustments accordingly. As a general rule, when interest rates are high and coming down, it is wise to invest in bonds. When interest rates are low and climbing, the stock market is the correct place to invest. When the prime rate is at 10 percent or lower, it is a favorable climate for the stock market. When the prime rate climbs above 10 percent, bonds are more favorable. Of course, there are other economic indicators that I use, being a professional analyst. But these rules provide a system easy enough for most investors to use.

The golden rule of investing is this: Invest in mutual funds that are going up and sell funds that are going down. It is as simple as can be, yet most people violate this principle because of emotions. For example, if your investment is dropping in value, the tendency is to want to stay in until things turn around and your losses are recovered. That's the wrong thing to do. You need to sell before you lose even more money. It may hurt your ego to sell for a little less than you bought, but it's better to bruise your ego than your portfolio.

Conversely, when an investment is rising in value, the tendency is to want to be greedy and refuse to sell, even when the fund goes down, hoping that it will go back up again. So the nagging question in either situation is, When do you sell? Obviously you should sell when it is most profitable, but it may be hard to pinpoint when that is.

Let me explain the golden rule of investing in more detail. The scientific principle of momentum is the basis for one of the best systems I have found for stripping out emotion and acting on logic for investment decisions. This is in accord with the law of inertia discovered by Sir Isaac Newton. His law states that an object in motion tends to keep moving in that same direction. Likewise, a stock, bond or mutual fund that is rising in value tends to continue to rise. One that is falling tends to keep falling.

In order to determine what constitutes the most true sense of falling or rising, a benchmark is needed. Once the security passes the benchmark, this signals a buy or sell decision.

The most commonly accepted benchmarks are the thirty-nine-week and thirteen-week moving averages. These represent the average price for the security over the previous thirty-nine and thirteen weeks. The averages at any one time represent a dot on the graphs. After charting this for several weeks and connecting the dots, the lines such as the gentle curves in the illustration in table 5 on page 99 can be created. The more irregular, jagged line is the actual price of this particular security index.

When the price line moves above the thirty-nine-week moving average, this signals a good time to buy. Accordingly, when the security drops below the line, this signals a good time to sell.

As you will see in the example, the system is not guaranteed always to be an accurate indicator, but it is extremely reliable in most market conditions.

This concept is employed by many of the nation's most popular experts at timing the market, including Martin Zweig, J.W. Dicks and Bill Donahue.

To assist you in following this and other systems, you may decide to subscribe to a market timing newsletter. One I highly recommend is the Mutual Fund Advisor, published by the J.W. Dicks Research Institute. For a free copy call (800) 333-3700. If you would like to sample some other market timing newsletters before subscribing, the Select Information Exchange offers you the opportunity to try fifteen different newsletters in its catalog for only $8. You will get between one and five issues of each newsletter, and the fee may be partially applied to the price of the sub-

Table 5

Moving Averages Compared to Actual Price for a Sample Security Index*

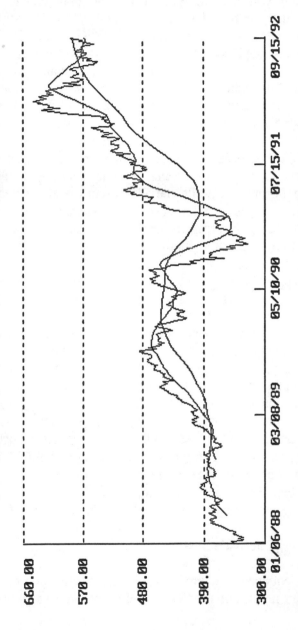

*The above chart is a price history of the NASDAQ Composite from January 1988 to September 1992. Data was derived from Warner Data Systems and graphed by James L. Paris Financial Services.

Notes: The jagged line represents the *actual price of a security*. The smooth, curved lines represent moving averages: the one that starts first being a *thirty-nine-week moving average*, and the other a *thirteen-week moving average*.

scription you eventually choose. You may contact the Select Information Exchange at 244 West Fifty-fourth Street, Suite 714, New York, NY 10019; (212) 247-7123.

For less sophisticated advice you can read various consumer and financial magazines, often available at your library. For example, *Money* magazine provides monthly performance rankings of various categories of funds as well as other good personal financial management articles.

Track record is so important in choosing a mutual fund that you should never invest in a new mutual fund. I recommend looking at a fund that has at least a ten-year favorable performance. While the advertisements are correct in saying that past performance is no guarantee of future results, the track record nevertheless gives quite a valuable indication of how the fund is handled. As Jesus said, you will know a tree by its fruits.

In appendix F I have listed twenty no-load and low-load mutual funds whose long-term track records are outstanding. In appendix G you will find a list of addresses and phone numbers that will allow you access to more than four hundred no-load/low-load funds. (Some companies listed have multiple funds.) Most of them have toll-free phone numbers and will be happy to send you a packet of information about how each fund in their family differs from others and what each one's investment strategy is. For the long-term savings strategies I am discussing, such as college and retirement, you will want a "growth fund." This means that while the dividends may not be the highest available, the value of the fund's stocks is expected to increase substantially over time, providing a strong return.

America's Best-kept Investment Secrets

I mentioned that most exotic investment opportunities are bad news, but I'd like to point out two exceptions to that rule: tax lien certificates and discounted mortgages.

Tax Lien Certificates

Suppose that I fail to pay $3,000 in property taxes. The county will send me dunning notices for about three months; then they will place a lien on my property. Once that lien is placed on my property, the county has prevented me from selling my home without paying the $3,000 in taxes.

However, if I don't plan to sell my home for a long time, then the county converts the lien into a certificate and auctions it off to an investor. The county plans to charge me interest on the lien, so investors bid on interest rates. In this instance the investor with the lowest bid — the lowest interest rate — wins the certificate.

In some states, county governments can charge up to 50 percent interest per year on property tax liens. In Florida, where I live, the top interest rate is 18 percent. So let's say an investor wins the bid at 16 percent interest and buys the certificate on my property. By auctioning off the certificate, the county collects the tax money due on the property. The investor pays the $3,000 to the county, and the county begins to levy the 16 percent interest on the lien against me, the property owner. I am supposed to pay the taxes plus interest at a rate of 16 percent, and the county turns the principal and interest payments over to the investor who bought the tax lien certificate. What often happens, of course, is that since I did not have money to pay taxes, I do not have money to pay interest on the lien, either. So the lien investor gets no income — until the county takes final action.

In Florida if the property owner is delinquent on property taxes for three years, the real estate is then auctioned off by the county. The investor will then receive his remaining principal balance plus interest because tax lien certificates are in a position of senior debt, meaning that the investor will be one of the first people paid when the property is sold.

Though unusual, these certificates are very good investments. You are almost guaranteed to receive your principal plus interest unless the property becomes totally worthless, which is not likely to happen.

I recently attended a tax lien certificate auction in Orange County, Florida, and noted that it was a very easy process. I interviewed the county tax collector after the auction, and he felt it was a great investment but that few people are aware of these auctions.

Tax lien certificates are available in most states. If you are interested in finding out more about them, call your county government offices and ask for the county tax collector's office.

Discounted Mortgages

A person selling a piece of real estate sometimes must provide some or all of the financing for the buyer. In the real estate chapter I will discuss seller financing, where a seller creates a second mortgage for the buyer by holding a note on a portion of the sale price of the home. While this is done occasionally to facilitate a sale, most sellers would rather have the cash up front than be paid over the life of the second mortgage. Herein lies the opportunity.

The person holding this second mortgage can sell it to an investor and receive cash. Investors are securing very good rates of return by finding people holding mortgages for a property they sold. It is a relatively easy process. By visiting your county courthouse you will find the records of mortgages. Anytime you see a mortgage being held by an individual, you can contact the people to see whether they are interested in selling the mortgage. You can also run an ad in the classified section of your newspaper, saying that you buy mortgages for cash.

Let's say that you find a person who has just provided a second mortgage for $10,000 at 8 percent interest for ten years. They will collect $121.33 per month from the borrower, but they would rather have their money now, in cash. You offer the owner of this note less than the face value, say $7,500. If they agree to this price, the borrower is still obligated to pay back $10,000. If you subtract your $7,500 from the $10,000 plus interest and recalculate the difference as interest on your $7,500 investment, you are effectively locking in a 15 percent rate of return on your investment. A friend of mine has been investing in discounted mortgages for years, and he has been able to negotiate prices where he ends up receiving as much as 35 percent interest.

Discounted mortgages are better known than the tax lien certificates, so you will have some competition. But it is possible to find mortgage holders who are anxious to get a lump sum payment, and they will discount the face value in order to receive that cash.

These two investment opportunities involve more work than investing in mutual funds, but they can be exciting opportunities if you have the time to explore them.

Summary

Beware of penny stocks. Forego collectibles for *investment purposes*. Buy jewelry, coins, baseball cards and other such items as hobbies and for the pleasure of ownership. Buy a time-share at a reduced price if you would like to use it for vacation purposes. Yes, there will be some residual value in any of these options, perhaps a lot. But don't fool yourself — you will probably never make a profit on them, so do not consider them investments.

Mutual funds offer a reasonable chance for excellent

long-term growth of your investment at minimal risk. Be patient with your investment, and you will see a good return. Also, be a good steward, monitoring your investment and the changes in the economy.

The parable of the talents teaches us about God's standard for money management. He deserves our very best. It is my hope that you have now set a higher standard for your investments and will make the most of what is truly God's money.

Questions

Why Mutual Funds?

Question: The 1990s offer the investor a confusing array of investment choices. Can you please reiterate why you prefer mutual funds over all the other possibilities, such as stocks, bonds, commodities and so on?

Answer: I have worked with literally thousands of people and have had the opportunity to see which investments have worked and which have not. Mutual funds stand out. The main reasons I like them:

• *They are easy to understand.* Many listeners to my radio program are immediately able to understand the concept of a mutual fund and get started.

• *They are completely liquid.* This means that in an emergency you can get your money out with just a twenty-four-hour notice in many cases.

• *They offer professional management.* Some of the brightest minds on Wall Street can be yours, such as the famed Peter Lynch, the former manager of the Fidelity Magellan Fund. Usually the fee for management is less than 1 percent per year.

• *They offer diversification.* The word *mutual* indicates that this kind of investment is for the mutual benefit of all who participate. Some mutual funds own more than one hundred different securities. This would not be possible for the small investor with $10,000; $20,000; or even $100,000. Pooling your money with other investors gives you tremendous diversification and, therefore, safety.

No other investment option I have found over the years provides all four of these benefits.

Mutual Fund Families

Question: What is a "family" of mutual funds?

Answer: "Family" means the mutual fund company offers numerous funds. The most simple version of this is the availability of a stock fund, a bond fund and a money market fund. Some fund families offer over eighty to ninety different funds.

Since 1970 there has been a vast increase in the choices of funds. Many fund groups offer not only international funds alongside their basic stock, bond and money market counterparts, but also specialized international funds, such as those investing in Europe or the Pacific Basin. The greater the amount of choice, the greater the benefit to the investor who wishes to follow markets closely and adjust a portfolio periodically.

Additionally, some fund families offer sector funds, which specialize in an industry, such as computer stocks. Such funds are still diversified in that they might own stock in twenty or thirty computer companies. But they are all in the same industry. Sector funds can provide great opportunities for those who wish to buy into specific industries.

Buy-and-Hold Versus Timing

Question: What is your opinion of the buy-and-hold strategy as opposed to moving averages or market timing?

Answer: Investing in a good mutual fund that has an outstanding track record and holding it will usually give you far greater results than bank savings accounts, certificates of deposit or other low-return investments. But for the ambitious investor, there are even higher returns to be made. By using a market timing system, as described in this chapter on investing, investors can make even more with their mutual funds than they would by simply buying and holding. When a mutual fund is showing a momentum of growth, buy it. Once it starts to show a downward momentum, sell it. But if you're not in a position to follow your mutual funds this closely, you may want to consider retaining an organization that will provide market timing services for you. An affiliate company of Financial Boot Camp for Christians, James L. Paris Financial Services [(800) 950-PLAN], provides this service.

Options and Futures
Question: What is your opinion of options and futures contracts?

Answer: One of my good friends says, "If you like to gamble, you'll probably have a better time on a cruise ship than you will investing in commodities, options and futures." Putting money into commodities, options and futures is not so much investing as it is gambling because you are simply betting, via a contract, that prices will move one way or the other. Yes, some people have made a lot of money in this area. However, it's very similar to the lottery — most people lose. A small percentage wins, and that small number of investors makes a tremendous amount of money.

On the other hand, commodities, options and futures may be used wisely as hedges against losing too much money in other investments. Let's say you own a stock. To protect yourself from losing too much money if that stock were to go down, you could buy an option to sell it at a certain price, almost like buying an insurance policy. Whoever bought your option would have to buy that stock at the contracted price if it dropped to that level. Many times farmers or people involved with commodities will buy commodities and futures contracts as an insurance against, say, having a bad year with their farm. Using these areas as hedges makes sense, but investing in them simply to make a profit tends to result in lost money.

Investing in Church Bonds

Question: My church is offering church bonds and encouraging us to invest our retirement funds and the funds we have set aside for a college education into these church bonds. The bonds will pay an attractive interest rate and, according to the pastor, will have a first mortgage position on the property. I'd like to help out my church, and at the same time I wouldn't mind making a good rate of return on my money. Do you see a problem with this type of investment?

Answer: Yes, I do have a problem with this type of investment. Many churches, with good intentions, will often finance an expansion through church bonds. A bond, simply stated, is an I.O.U. You give your money to the church, and they promise to pay you back with a prescribed interest rate. Also, your bond is collateralized. That is, the church bond has a lien against the real estate, just as the bank that loaned you money when you purchased your home has a lien against your home as well.

The reason churches go to their congregations for the financing and not to a bank is because they are not creditworthy enough to get bank financing. A bank would look at things such as income, revenue and the ability to repay to determine the risk of the loan. Unless the church has been around for a long time and has a good revenue stream, it may be difficult for them to qualify unless they have a large down payment for the project.

By the way, I think it is a good idea for the church to

save up a substantial amount of money to put down so that they can get conventional bank financing. I don't have a problem with people giving to a church building fund. I certainly think it's biblical that we give to the Lord's work and help our church. But I don't believe in mixing charitable giving with investing.

Churches do go bankrupt. I've heard of elderly people who have put retirement funds into church bonds because they wanted to help the church out. That was money they had set aside to draw income from during retirement. Then the church failed, and the property was sold at auction. They were given back less than the amount of money they had invested. I would much rather have seen them give a $10,000 gift to the building fund than to invest their $100,000 and get back less than $60,000 or $70,000 because of the default on the bonds. It is irresponsible for church administrations to advertise church bonds as a no-risk opportunity for funding college education or retirement. Yet on several occasions I have heard of churches advertising church bonds as virtually guaranteed. I strongly object to this because it is misleading.

If you are going to loan money to your church, do what a bank would do. I would want to review financial statements. I would also want to bring in a trained financial planner to evaluate them as well. Be very careful not to mix your charitable intentions with investing.

Tax Lien Investing

Question: How can I learn more about tax lien investing?

Answer: Contact your county tax collector's office. Usually someone there will help you understand the process. They are always looking for investors who are willing to purchase tax lien certificates so the county can receive its needed revenue. An additional resource you may want to consider is a tax lien auction video that Financial Boot Camp has developed. For more information, call us at (800) 877-2022.

Time-share Condos

Question: Unfortunately, I purchased a time-share unit before I read your materials. What do I do with it now? Is there any possible way I can sell this?

Answer: Only about 3 percent of all time-share owners have been successful in reselling their units. There are organizations promising quick sales of time-share units. Traditionally they request a listing fee of $150 to $500 and a 10 percent commission *if* they sell the unit. They will then list your property in a computer data bank and supposedly try to sell it for you. Unfortunately, the numbers prove that these organizations make the majority of their money from the listing fees and not from selling the properties. Be very wary of time-share resale organizations.

My best advice: If you own a time-share unit, get your money's worth out of it. You've already made a mistake. Don't make a second one by trying to sell it and paying hefty fees and probably not having a very successful experience doing so. Learn everything you can about that time-share, such as how you can exchange it and how you can save the week if you decide not to use it in a given year. Many people who own time-shares have a fantastic time each year vacationing in Hawaii or Europe.

If you'd like to find out more about time-share resale and about time-shares in general, contact the Resort Property Owners of America at 175 West Jackson, Suite 1901 Chicago, IL 60604; (800) 446-7762.

EIGHT

THE LAND MINE
OF SCHEMES
AND SCAMS

A man with an evil eye hastens after riches.
Proverbs 28:22 (NKJV)

*E**vil eye* can be translated as "selfish motives." A man with selfish motives has a goal of getting rich quick, and thus he falls prey to every kind of dishonest scheme.

Christians are not excluded. In fact, Christians tend to be overly susceptible to scams. I don't understand why — perhaps it is because we are trusting individuals. We are mindful of other's needs and have a willingness to love our neighbors. Sometimes our openness leaves us wide open to be victims.

As I have talked with individuals about this topic, I have seen which investment opportunities make money and which ones do not. Many people learn about scams the hard way — they learn to safeguard their finances and invest carefully only after they have become victims. The purpose of this chapter is to help you avoid the land mines of schemes and scams and to make you a wary investor.

A maxim the U.S. Postal Service coined years ago still holds true and not just for deals offered through the mail: "If it sounds too good to be true, it probably is." Abraham Lincoln once said, "You can fool some of the people all of the time, and all of the people some of the time, but you cannot fool all of the people all of the time."

Questionable and outright fraudulent schemes are so prevalent that on my national radio program I have a regular feature called "The Scam of the Week." I alert my listeners to the latest offers which may not be legitimate. Let's look at some of the categories that continually surface.

Advance Fee Loan Scam

One of the biggest recent scams is the advance fee loan scam. Operators will run classified ads in major newspapers, national magazines or tabloids. They offer loans of up to $50,000 or $100,000, regardless of your credit history. You are to send them a fee of $20 to $100, and they will furnish you with an application for the loan. In many cases the consumer will never hear from the company again. These companies have neither the intention nor the ability to loan money. They simply collect their application fees and disappear. The Federal Trade Commission is in the process of investigating these operators in an effort to shut them down.

Home Employment Scam

In an effort to stay on top of some of the schemes currently making the rounds, I have ordered some of the products in this category. Some ads say that you can make

$40,000 a year stuffing envelopes from home, and for $10 you can receive an information packet which tells you how to earn the money. So I sent my $10, and, just as I suspected, the information told me to run a similar ad in newspapers. By charging a fee for the information packet, which simply instructs others to do the same, I could collect up to $40,000 a year in fees. This, of course, is an illegal pyramid scheme, which I will discuss later in this chapter.

Another ad I investigated promised me an income of $50,000 a year from reading books at home.

I sent them $30, and in return I received a twenty-page pamphlet. This pamphlet listed the names and addresses of publishers and newspapers along with a sample form letter for me to send to each of these companies to see whether I could be hired as an outside consultant to review materials they were considering publishing. Obviously I didn't get much for my $30 investment, and I could have gotten the list of publishers and newspapers for free from the library.

These sales pitches come in many forms, often offering nothing more than information that could easily be obtained for free. Once you get on their mailing list, don't be surprised if you are solicited regularly with all types of different offers. In the words of P.T. Barnum, "A sucker is born every minute." Once you appear gullible to these companies, they will try to exploit you with every possible direct mail or telemarketing campaign.

Mail-Order Scams

I have had U.S. postal inspectors as guests on my radio program. They informed my audience that mail-order scams are not limited to the financial category. There are many products advertised, especially for weight loss, which do not live up to their claims. Many pills, creams and other products promise fast, effortless weight loss. I am not saying all diet products and systems are scams. But if you are not sure about which ones are legitimate, some research in health and consumer magazines can acquaint you with the proven providers.

One problem with mail-order scams is that once the products are delivered, it is almost impossible to get a refund. Many of these mail-order companies are out of business shortly after running their ads. Mail-order companies often use post office boxes for addresses, so they are very difficult to trace.

I asked one inspector how fraudulent companies can run ads for products and services that are obviously flawed and not get caught. He said the Postal Service occasionally may catch a scam artist, fine him and shut his business down. But within weeks the same person will have reincorporated in another state under another name and will start the scam all over again.

It is always best to do business with mail-order companies that are well known and that have good reputations for fast service and prompt refunds.

Credit Scams

One classified ad claimed that I could get up to $100,000 in credit with just my signature. The advertiser promised to teach me a "little known strategy" for wiping out all my debts without going into bankruptcy. To investigate further I purchased the information. The booklet that was sent to me was filled with unethical practices and outright fraud. For example, it encouraged me to take advantage of a Federal Trade Commission regulation designed to protect the consumer from faulty merchandise. It urged me to invoke this regulation for each purchase made in the last two to three years and to complain to the FTC that these products were not all that they claimed to be. I supposedly would receive a refund from these companies and therefore be able to pay off my debts. Whether this strategy works or not, this type of deceit should be out of the question for the Christian consumer.

Another scheme for dealing with debt was to postpone payment by sending the creditor a check without signing it. The creditor will send it back, thinking it was an honest error, and generally the consumer will not be penalized for a late payment. However, this is highly unethical, and the creditor will catch on fast if this strategy is used every month. Furthermore, it doesn't make the bills go away.

Several other suggestions were along this line of tampering with checks. I won't even detail them because they are illegal and therefore hardly worth the mention.

What is the common thread of these products? "If it sounds too good to be true, it probably is." These are true consumer land mines. If you were in battle and stepped on a land mine, you generally wouldn't know what hit you. People can work their entire lives to build up savings and equity, and within an instant they can lose it all if they are caught up in an unscrupulous scheme.

Lottery Scams

Many scams exist in which one person outwits another out of his money through fast talking and believable stories. One of the most popular scams involves lottery tickets, an envelope of cash found unexpectedly or similar alleged windfalls. These scams thrive in large cities, where many ethnic groups are represented.

The lottery scam usually involves a person of ethnic origin, who will approach a person of similar origin — often an elderly person believed to have savings that can be easily withdrawn — and claim to hold a winning lottery ticket worth thousands of dollars. The con artist says he would like to collect, but being an illegal alien and without a Social Security number, he is ineligible for the prize. The con man tries to persuade the victim to collect the winnings, and, in return, they will split the money.

The scam artist asks the victim to give him several thousand dollars in cash of good faith money in exchange for the winning ticket. The scam artist sends the victim alone to claim the prize. Of course by the time the ticket is found to be worthless, the scam artist is gone with the victim's cash.

The moral to that type of story is that if you wish to help a stranger, do so without expecting anything in return or you may find yourself outwitted by a clever scam.

Multilevel Marketing

Whenever I conduct a seminar, people ask if multilevel marketing is a scam. A true multilevel marketing firm is not a scam. Richard DeVos, president and cofounder of the Amway Corporation, is a fine Christian and is also the brains behind what we know today as multilevel marketing. In order to qualify in this category, products or services must be part of the marketing effort. If the company is simply selling memberships with no products or services to offer, this is known as a pyramid scheme, which is illegal in this country.

In a pyramid the most recent investor's money is used to pay the investors already in the organization (the pinnacle of the pyramid). Therefore, more and more investors are needed to keep the scam alive (at the broadening base of the pyramid). Once no more investors can be found, the pyramid crumbles and shuts down. Many people have lost thousands of dollars through this type of scam. Envision the workings of a chain letter that asks for money, and you have a pyramid scheme in a nutshell.

I have two criticisms of true multilevel marketing operations. One is that they tend to overrepresent the value of the business opportunity and make it sound so simple, when, in fact, building this type of business takes great dedication and hours of hard work. Not everyone is gifted in sales and the other skills needed to succeed in multilevel marketing. Also, some such organizations have been known to recruit members by promising great riches, in effect pandering to covetousness, which is contrary to biblical values.

Second, many Christians who get involved in these businesses become so zealous — or desperate — that they try to recruit from within their local church. They may alienate people coming into the church by making them feel that they are nothing more than prospective customers.

Recognize also that most multilevel companies decide to market their products through networking because they do not have the money to buy local and national advertising to sell their products. Or, to put it more favorably, they put their marketing savings into commissions for the salesperson and the hierarchy over him or her. Of course, this means the pressure is on the salespeople and managers to expand the market continually with their own efforts.

The downside of marketing this way is that there is great risk of these companies going out of business. You should only join multilevel marketing firms that have a proven track record and that plan to stay in business.

Do your homework. Research multilevel marketing companies through your state attorney general's office and your Better Business Bureau. Also, you need to ask the multilevel company's representative questions such as these:

• How long has your company been in business?

• I would like to try your products first before I join to see if they are all that you advertise them to be. Can you provide me with free samples?

• Can you provide me with some names of *local* people

who have been successful in this business, not just the few millionaires this company has made?

• How do you arrive at the pricing of the products, and can you substantiate your claims that I will save money by buying these products?

• Who is your competition? How do their products compare, both in price and quality?

• How many other distributors are there in this local area? Are there so many that the market is already saturated?

• Will I be trained to recruit other people and sell products, or am I left on my own once I have bought a distributorship?

• Must I meet a minimum quota each month in order to get my commissions, or can I take time off for a while and still receive the residual commissions owed to me? How often will the standards for achieving goals be adjusted?

• If I want to get out of the business, can I sell my interest to another person? If I die, can my business be transferred to a family member, along with the network I have already built?

• Does your business primarily promote itself by appealing to people's greedy and materialistic nature, promising they will get rich if they work with this company?

Multilevel marketing is a legitimate sales structure, but it is just as time-consuming and difficult to get going as any other small business.

Protecting Yourself

Get-rich-quick schemes abound by the thousands, and most are fraudulent or unworkable. Whether you are considering involvement in a multilevel marketing organization, opening a franchise or embarking on some other business investment, get as much information on the company as possible.

There are several ways you can go about this. Contact the consumer affairs office or the attorney general's office in the capital of the state in which the business is incorporated. They can tell you whether the business is under any type of investigation.

Once you have determined that the business is clear of investigations, contact the Better Business Bureau in the city where the business is based. The BBB is simply an information data base of complaints on businesses. It is not a policing organization, though it can send information to the attorney general's office. The BBB can send you a printout of all the information on file for the business you are interested in.

If the investment is out of your field of experience, say in real estate, you should consult with someone in that field who can review any information you have obtained and advise you as to whether it is a wise investment.

Ask the business for referrals of customers. If they are not willing to provide these referrals from happy customers, chances are that they don't have any.

In the end, if you have any doubts about the company, don't proceed with the investment.

A man who called in on my radio show thought he was purchasing a franchise to sell teddy bears. He flew to Beverly Hills, California, visited the offices and, after the tour, wrote a $13,000 check to get into the business. One week later the company was out of business and the investor was out his money. I asked if he had done some of the investigative work I have detailed here, and he had not.

If you feel you have been scammed, it is important to report the incident. Contact the Federal Trade Commission, specifically the FTC's Bureau of Consumer Protection, at (202) 326-3128. If it involves a mail-order scam, contact the Postal Crime Hotline at (800) 654-8896.

You can also try to resolve your dispute with a company through a small claims court. Depending on the state, small claims courts handle cases with a value less than $5,000. In most cases you do not need an attorney, and the costs will usually be less than $100. Essentially it is two people discussing their differences with a judge, similar to television's "The People's Court." A small claims court may provide the leverage you need to recover your losses from a disreputable business.

It is biblical for Christians to make every effort to resolve differences short of going to court. But in the case of a loss involving a business, court may be your best alternative.

We can't look to the government to shut down all the unethical businesses that exist. They cannot protect us from our own carelessness or greed. We must take some personal responsibility for our naiveté in wanting to believe that these schemes will make us rich.

There are no true get-rich-quick schemes. You can obtain wealth *slowly* through using the investment principles detailed in this book by putting away money each month. God wants to protect you from making a mistake that will adversely affect your financial future. So commit your investments to prayer, and ask the Holy Spirit to protect you from unscrupulous investments.

Questions

Financial Fraud

Question: I feel that I've been defrauded by a financial company in a transaction. What should I do?

Answer: Contact a manager or salesperson at the office and explain the situation. Allow them approximately five business days to resolve the problem. If the problem is not resolved to your satisfaction, contact the corporate headquarters in writing and allow them five business days to respond with a satisfactory solution.

In most cases this problem will be resolved at least by the time it gets to the corporate headquarters because insurance companies and other financial entities are highly regulated; the last thing they want is a complaint to a regulatory agency. However, as a last resort, contact your state's department of regulation for that industry.

For example, if it's a stock brokerage, contact your state's division of securities. If it is an insurance company, contact your state's division of insurance. If it's a bank, contact your state's division of banking and finance. In most cases, by filing a complaint with a regulatory agency, you will definitely get the company's attention and eventually a fair resolution.

NINE

THE LAND MINE
OF INSURANCE

The rain came down, the streams rose,
and the winds blew and beat against that house;
yet it did not fall, because
it had its foundation on the rock.
Matthew 7:25

Long before a prominent insurance company adopted the concept of stability in a rock, Jesus used this word to describe a right relationship with Him. This illustration also paints a vivid picture of families with proper insurance planning when the storms of life rage.

As we strive to be good stewards of the money with which God has blessed us, insurance is an area that can be especially tricky. The concept is simple enough — it is the clever packaging by the insurance industry that has made it especially difficult for consumers to make informed decisions.

In this chapter I am going to talk about various types of insurance. I will focus on life insurance because this is the area most misunderstood. Too many people are easily sold a product that does not fit their needs.

121

Life Insurance

In my speaking engagements I have been aggressively challenged about my opinions on insurance, particularly on life insurance. It seems that the life insurance industry has convinced its salespeople to believe that their skewed, though highly profitable, approach to life insurance is the only right way to address this basic need.

"The life insurance industry has become a voracious octopus, squeezing the financial life's blood out of millions of American families," says insurance expert Arthur Milton, author of the book *How Your Life Insurance Policies Rob You*.

The rationale for life insurance is simple. If a breadwinner in a family dies, the surviving spouse and children would be forced to struggle without the deceased's income. Life insurance is intended to replace the breadwinner's income so that needs are met, whether the survivors include a working spouse, a nonworking spouse or no spouse at all.

Who needs life insurance? In my opinion single persons do not need life insurance. As for children, it is a waste of money to insure their lives beyond the cost of funeral expenses, which average $5,000 to $10,000 nationally. And, finally, life insurance is a concept designed for your younger years. There should be no need for it when you are old.

How much life insurance is enough? Most people have some life insurance but don't have any idea what a reasonable amount would be to meet their family's needs. For example, $100,000 may sound like a great deal of money, but when you compare that figure to your potential income over the next twenty to thirty years, $100,000 is a small fraction.

The easiest way to calculate your life insurance needs is to multiply your current monthly expenses by twelve to get a yearly figure. This is the income your family needs to maintain the standard of living you presently have. Then multiply that yearly figure, say $36,000, by ten. If all that expense is being met by one spouse's income, the amount of life insurance needed for that spouse would be $360,000. When the money is invested, a 10 percent rate of return would provide your current expenses — $36,000 a year.

You may also need to consider the expenses of replacing the domestic services of a nonworking spouse (such as child care, cooking, cleaning and so on). When you arrive at this figure, you should also multiply it by ten to determine the amount of life insurance to buy for this person.

When calculating your total monthly expenses, keep in mind that your need for income may also be reduced somewhat upon the death of an adult family member. For example, you may be able to eliminate one of your automobiles and its related costs. In addition, a young, nonworking wife who is widowed may want to get a full-time job when her children reach high school age, thus providing other income. So the figures here may be somewhat conservative.

My example relies on a rate of return of 10 percent. Of course, a lower rate of return would mean less income or would require a dip into the principal amount.

The only reasonably priced life insurance product on the market today is term insurance. Term insurance is usually purchased on a yearly basis, thus the name *term*. The most popular form is called A.R.T. — annual renewable term insurance. This insurance is guaranteed renewable, and I would recommend it. As the policyholder ages, the rate of the insurance increases because aging increases the chance of death.

Adjoining this concept of term life insurance is the concept that people in their sixties and seventies should not need life insurance. If they have planned for their finances in retirement and have paid off all their debts, including their home, the need for life insurance dwindles to no need at all. Therefore, as the price of the insurance increases, eventually you can cancel the policy, provided you have planned well.

As Christians we want to be good stewards with our money and make arrangements for our family should we die prematurely. One way to improve stewardship is to study your life insurance policies. You should probably replace any nonterm products with term insurance.

Certain types of life insurance are very expensive. Here are some you should avoid:

Credit Life Insurance

I recently closed on a loan for a home refinancing, and I had to sit through the loan officer's pitch for credit life insurance. This is the biggest rip-off in the insurance industry. It is extremely overpriced and is simply a way for insurance companies to make easy money.

Credit life insurance seems to be offered on just about every credit product today — automobile loans, credit cards — you name it. The concept of credit life insurance is good: If the borrower should die before the loan is paid, the policy pays the balance.

The presentation I got for credit life insurance was smoother than most — I even received a color brochure. It stated that credit life insurance was "inexpensive — only 60 cents for every $100 borrowed." This may sound cheap, but if you compare this rate to a simple term insurance policy on the borrower, this credit life insurance is priced at up to *eight times* the cost of term insurance.

In addition, the credit life premium never decreases, even though the principal balance on the loan decreases. For example, if you borrowed $10,000 originally, and the credit life premium was $6 per thousand (or $60 per year), when the principal balance is paid down to $1,000, you are still paying the premium of $60 per year for the insurance. This means that instead of $6 per thousand, you are paying $60 per thousand! This policy of overpricing is the only reason I don't like credit life insurance. If you presently have this insurance on *any* credit product, cancel it immediately. If necessary, replace it with inexpensive term life insurance.

Life insurance is important, but there are better ways to protect your loan obligations than buying credit life insurance.

Cash Value Insurance

Over the past one hundred years, the insurance industry has misled more American consumers than any scheme or scam by selling one of the worst values in America today: cash value life insurance. Cash value insurance has several different varieties. The best known is called whole life insurance. As the name suggests, this insurance is designed to cover you for your whole life. This is accomplished by considerably overcharging an individual when he is young to provide for lower premiums when the individual ages. With the vanishing premium plan, you pay on the policy of a period of, say, ten years. The insurance company invests these high premiums and makes a profit on them, and eventually part of that interest income they receive will go toward the payment of your premium.

Whole life insurance policies also allow your insurance agent to earn eight to ten times the commissions he would earn if he recommended you buy term insurance. The biggest part of the sales pitch to buy whole life insurance is that it will be too expensive for you to buy insurance when you are older if you have a term insurance policy. But, remember, *you should not need life insurance when you are old.* Life insurance is designed to replace the loss of income from the death of a wage earner when at least one survivor still depends on those wages. Yet most retired individuals do not work but receive income from pensions, investments and Social Security. These sources of income continue, in most cases, for the surviving spouse.

The term *cash value* is misleading as well. While your insurance policy does have some value, it is not even close to the amount of money you have poured into it. Surrender value is what you receive if you cash in the policy, and it is usually a small amount.

It is also a bad idea to borrow against your insurance policy. In the first place, it is your money you are borrowing because you have paid the premiums, yet the insurance company will charge you interest on the loan. Imagine paying interest on your own money! Second, this decreases the value of the life insurance product. If you have a $100,000 life insurance policy and borrow $30,000 against it, the policy will be worth only $70,000 if the policyholder dies.

Universal life insurance is another cash value product. It is slightly better than whole life insurance because it splits up the investment section of the insurance more definitively. The company applies a certain amount of your premium toward the life insurance segment of the policy, and the balance will go into an investment account. The catch is that the insurance company makes tremendous returns on your money by greatly overcharging you for life insurance, while giving you a small rate of return on the investment side.

If you like the concept of whole life or universal life insurance, it is possible to build your own policy. For example, let's say your insurance agent says that a universal life policy for $100,000 will cost you $100 per month. The agent also tells you that an annual renewable term insurance policy for the same face value is $20 per month. Buy the term insurance for $20 per month, and then find an acceptable investment, such as a no-load mutual fund or a mutual fund annuity, and put $80 into the fund each month. In essence you have duplicated what the insurance company would provide, without paying the high commissions or fees to that insurance company.

For more information you can also call Financial Boot Camp for Christians at (800) 877-2022. For a small fee we will provide you with a computer printout of more than 350 insurance companies and the best rates for your situation. We don't sell insurance, so we can be totally unbiased. Also, two organizations offering no-load (no commission) life insurance policies are Ameritas [(800) 552-3553] and USAA [(800) 292-8000].

Health Insurance

Most people secure health insurance at their place of employment through group plans. The rates are spread over a large number of people, keeping them relatively low. However, if you are self-employed and purchase insurance outside of a group situation, the rates can be astronomical. There are solutions to this problem. Consumer advocate Ralph Nader, appearing on my radio program, advised that if you are not currently part of a group because of self-employment, you need to join a group — perhaps a chamber of commerce or trade association that fits your small business. These organizations often have health insurance plans you can buy into.

Generally, when you are part of a group, most states do not allow the insurance company to discriminate against you in terms of rates. Group rates are set by looking at a wide range of persons and illnesses, and each individual within that group is charged the same amount. If you buy insurance individually, the insurance company can charge you higher rates for certain medical conditions you may have. So the concept of shared group risk is best because the group is large enough to be representative of the insurance company's research on the number of claims they can expect.

If you are having difficulty fitting health insurance into your budget, you may want to opt for major medical coverage. There is usually a $1,000 deductible, with 80/20 coinsurance. This means that after you pay the first $1,000 in charges, the insurance company will pay 80 percent of the subsequent bills, while you are responsible for the remaining 20 percent. There is also usually a stop-loss coverage, which means you will pay up to a certain dollar figure before the insurance company pays 100 percent of all bills. If this is the only coverage you can afford, it is by far the most important because it covers the catastrophic illnesses that can financially ruin a family.

Additionally, if you have trouble finding a group situation for health insurance, contact your state's division of insurance because many states are now providing low-cost health insurance for people who have their own businesses.

The cost of health care has skyrocketed out of sight and, along with it, the cost of health insurance. There are more problems with the industry today than I can address here. But to illustrate the complexities, the potential unfairness and the need for diligence on your part to be aware of your present and future coverage, consider this example.

You are injured while employed (either on or off the job); but because you have insurance through your company policy, you have no problems paying for treatment. Later, you are laid off. When you find a new employer, that employer's insurance company can deny coverage to you regarding your area of injury because it is considered a pre-existing condition.

I saw a national news story that focused on this same problem. A family's daughter was diagnosed with cancer while the father was employed. The father lost his job, and after he was hired elsewhere, the new employer's insurance company refused to give coverage to the daughter because her cancer was a pre-existing condition. Many people are afraid to leave or lose their present jobs because of the difficulty they will have in obtaining health insurance.

I am sure we will see many changes to our health care system in the next few years as our country deals with the high cost of medical care. The wise consumer will monitor his own situation in light of industry changes.

Home Owner's Insurance

Normally, you should insure your house for about 80 percent of its value. Why not 100 percent? Because if your home burned down, the land would still be usable. Generally the insurance company will assess 80 percent of a home's value to the structure, 20 percent to the land. So be sure that you do not buy too much insurance.

Second, insure the contents for replacement value rather than actual value. If a thief steals your big-screen television that you paid $1,300 for three years ago, actual value insurance will figure in the depreciation cost of that item, and you will not be able to replace that television with the money the insurance company gives you for it. Replacement value insurance costs more, but it pays the amount that it would cost to replace the item, regardless of its age.

Automobile Insurance

Less is better when it applies to options within most automobile insurance policies. The bells and whistles of insurance coverage are usually overpriced. Automobile insurance salespeople can make dramatically higher commissions when they encourage you to buy unnecessary additional coverage or when they persuade you to go with low deductibles and, therefore, higher premiums.

Choosing your levels of deductibles is one of the biggest controls you have over the cost of auto insurance. If you raise your automobile deductibles to $500 for things such as collision and comprehensive losses (fire, vandalism, theft), in most policies you can reduce your premium by 25 percent. By raising that same deductible to $1,000 you can reduce your premium by as much as 50 percent.

Let's say you have a five-year-old auto, for which you paid $10,000 when it was new. That automobile is worth about $2,000. If you are carrying collision insurance, and the car is in an accident that "totals" the car, meaning that it would cost more to repair the car than it is worth, the insurance company will give you only today's value for that car, approximately $2,000. Obviously that car was worth more than $2,000 to you.

So when your automobile reaches about $2,000 in value or less and the car is paid off, drop the collision coverage. Collision covers only your car, not your liability for damage to other people's property. Collision coverage is usually expensive and not worth the money on older cars.

I am often asked how much liability coverage a person should have with an auto policy. Liability insurance pays for the damage you do to another person or that person's property. Liability coverage is required in most states. I would recommend that you purchase about two and a half times your net worth in liability coverage. In this lawsuit-happy society, it is not uncommon to read about huge awards being granted to people through automobile accident cases.

I recommend that people buy the minimum allowable liability coverage and then reinsure that automobile policy through an umbrella policy, which is very inexpensive liability coverage. I recommend $1 million as a good minimum, but if two and a half times your net worth is more than $1 million, increase your coverage accordingly. This policy will also cover your home owner's policy. Keep in mind, however, that the insurance company will probably want to provide you with both your home owner's and auto insurance before they will sell you the umbrella policy. The umbrella policy then picks up the liability from your home or auto policy when that coverage is used up.

It is wise to shop around for automobile insurance. Rates can vary widely from company to company, and even from state to state. You may spend some extra time on the phone, but you will save money.

Disability Insurance

Generally speaking, I am not a big advocate of disability insurance. Most of these policies are overpriced, and it can be very difficult to collect on them. Insurance companies make the regulations so stringent that it is a hassle to make a claim. I believe that the best way to handle disability coverage is to set aside three to six months' worth of living expenses and thus self-insure rather than pay the high cost of disability insurance. By self-insure I mean establish a savings program to build up your own fund for such an emergency. Most disabilities do not take someone out of the work force permanently, so you do not need to build up a gigantic fund.

I know people who have had good experiences with disability insurance and say that without it they would not have survived economically. But the large majority of my clients have not had such positive experiences.

One of the factors to consider is the elimination period. This is a period of usually one to six months during which you must be disabled before you can start collecting on the policy. These months, in essence, are "on you." Even though you have to cover your own costs during this time, I would recommend a longer elimination period so that the premiums are lower.

Second, look closely at the definition of disability. There are two critical terms here: *your occupation* and *any occupation*. *Your occupation* means that if you become unable to perform in the field in which you worked prior to the injury, then the insurance company pays you after the elimination period has passed.

However, *any occupation* insurance covers you only if you are totally disabled and not able to perform *any* type of work, regardless of your previous occupation. I would highly discourage even considering this type of insurance. You and I know that a tight-fisted insurance company will find some type of job that you could do, regardless of how satisfying it is or how well it pays.

I would also recommend you call your state's department of insurance and research the complaint history of a company before you buy disability insurance. Talk to friends or neighbors who have had positive experiences with disability policies and research the companies they used.

Summary

Buy only term life insurance. Get enough to cover ten times your annual salary. Join a group health care insurance plan, though it may take some research to find one if you are self-employed. Insure your home and land for no more than 80 percent of its replacement value (or 100 percent of the replacement value of the building). Consider an umbrella liability policy to supplement your home owner's and car insurance liability. Spend some time weighing your options in car insurance, especially deductibles, and don't carry collision insurance on an old car. You may want to consider building your own fund for disability instead of carrying disability insurance.

Questions

Cash Value Life Insurance

Question: I understand your feelings about whole life insurance. But what is so wrong with the concept of buying life insurance and at the same time having an investment value building up? It seems to me to be very convenient and easy to make one payment each month rather than buying term insurance and also buying a mutual fund. State your position on why you believe term life insurance is better than whole life and why I should invest my money outside of life insurance policies.

Answer: I don't have a problem with the idea of sending one payment off and having it pay for both an investment and an insurance policy. My problem is that the insurance industry has created a tremendous incentive — as much as eight to ten times the commission — for the salesperson who sells you whole life or cash value life insurance versus a term policy. I don't like the high fees and commissions associated with a product that does not constitute a good overall investment.

If someone were to create a cash value life insurance policy with low expenses and a fair rate of return to the investor, I would probably be one of the first to endorse it because I think the idea of convenience does make a lot of sense. Unfortunately the insurance industry will probably never make that available because there is such a high profit margin in expensive, high-commission whole life and cash value life insurance.

Remember, it's not that difficult to make an investment payment. You can, in many cases, ask your mutual fund company to take the money directly out of your checking account by using an electronic transfer of funds. Most mutual fund companies listed in this book will take money out of your checking account for no fee and move it electronically into your mutual fund account. Thus there is no need for you to do monthly paperwork.

Insuring a Nonworking Spouse

Question: Does a nonworking spouse need to be covered by life insurance?

Answer: If there are children involved, the answer is a definite yes. If the services of the homemaker had to be replaced, the costs would be substantial. Imagine hiring someone to care for three children, clean the house and clothes, prepare the meals and perform a host of other projects. The working spouse, usually the husband, could not add these sixty-plus hours to his weekly schedule.

Determine what it would cost to replace these services and multiply this by a factor of eight to ten. For example, if you determine that the cost of a housekeeper and nanny would be $20,000 per year, you need to have $160,000 to $200,000 in term life insurance on your nonworking spouse so that the money could earn a 10 percent return to cover the expenses of keeping up the home.

Umbrella Liability

Question: What is an umbrella liability policy? Is this a good idea?

Answer: This policy is designed to pay a liability judgment in the event that you are successfully sued for more than you are covered for by automobile or home owner liability coverage. Typically most insurance companies will sell you this coverage only if you have both your home and auto coverage with them. Once you've met a required minimum on each of these policies, you can purchase an inexpensive umbrella liability policy. I purchased $1 million of liability coverage for just $150. This is a tremendous savings for two reasons:

• If I were to increase the amount of liability on my automobile and home owner's insurance to $1 million, I would have paid several hundred dollars, not just $150.

• Umbrella liability covers all kinds of liability and even includes some aspects of your professional liability.

So the best way to insure yourself against liability is to keep the lowest possible liability coverage that you can on your home owner's insurance and your automobile insurance. Again, keep in mind that your insurance company will restrict how low you can go on those policies and still be allowed to buy the umbrella liability coverage. They understand this strategy very well and want you to buy a minimum amount of liability coverage for the home and the auto before they allow you to buy the inexpensive umbrella liability coverage.

One word of caution: Check with your state to find out what the minimum required liability coverage is for your automobile because you will be required to carry that even if your insurance company would allow you to buy less.

TEN

THE LAND MINE OF RENTING A HOUSE

As for me and my house, we will serve the Lord.
Joshua 24:15 (KJV)

Through my work I have found that the most successful investment is in an individual's home. I could tell you stories of phenomenal appreciation, such as someone who bought a house in Boston thirty years ago for $10,000 and sold it for about $350,000.

Owning your own home is the best investment you can ever make for two reasons. First, real estate has historically outperformed many other investment options. Second, you have to live somewhere; therefore, it makes sense to buy rather than rent your home so that you can enjoy an investment while it works for you.

People have many misconceptions about buying real estate. When I first moved to the Orlando, Florida, area, I remember making the decision to buy my first property. I had just gotten out of college, and I was looking for my first real job. I didn't have much money. But I knew that I didn't want to rent, and I didn't want to live in my parents' home. My remaining option was to purchase property.

Relatives told me, "You can't buy your own home...You're only twenty-one years old...You don't have enough money in the bank...You haven't been at your job long enough." They came up with more and more reasons why I could not buy a home. However, in about three weeks I had proven them wrong. My down payment was less than $500, and the owner financed my loan, a process I will discuss later.

You may have rented your lodging for years and given up all hope of being a home owner. But with some knowledge and planning you can probably arrange to buy your first home. Let's see what is involved.

How to Get Started

Ownership of that first home has always been the major financial step for most Americans. Owning property brings with it a great deal of security and contentment. A monthly mortgage payment can, however, be a source of great stress if not carefully worked into a budget. I am going to look at the variables in a residential real estate purchase, how to determine how much of a home you can afford and, most important, how you can buy your first home (or next home).

The first thing to do is to establish your "must list." Before you even visit your first property or explore financing, write down some particulars, such as:

• What type of property would I like? A condominium or town house, where the outside maintenance is done by others (for a fee), or a house with a yard, which I must maintain?

• What do I want in a home? How many bedrooms, baths

and other amenities?
- What part of town will I live in?
- What price range is reasonable, based on my income and my housing preference?
- What can I afford for a down payment?
- Is my credit rating going to hamper the financing process?

Certain aspects you will be flexible about — perhaps whether a house is one or two levels or the degree of traffic on the road where it is located. But you need to draw up a must list in writing so that you can narrow your search and have a true picture of your housing needs and what you can afford.

Finding the Right Property

The best way to look for a home is to start backward. By this I mean that you should disqualify as many properties as you can in order to zero in on the few properties that fit your criteria. In other words, if you would like a four-bedroom home and a friend says he knows of a great three-bedroom home that you would really love, don't even consider it. If you do you will be compromising your must list and wasting valuable time.

You should research about fifty to seventy-five houses to make a truly informed purchase, sometimes even more, depending on your market. "Shop 'til you drop" will never pay off more than when buying a home. Don't look at homes you cannot afford (either because of the price of the home or the unacceptable financing arrangements) or homes that do not have the amenities you desire. The opportunity is out there for you to buy your first home and stop renting, but it is a challenge that can be met only by a determined individual.

How Much Can You Afford?

This question is not easy to answer. You may hear rules of thumb such as, "You can afford a home that would equal two and a half times your annual income," but this is simply painting with too broad a brush.

Let's start with the premise that you can afford the level of rent you are now paying — but how much more? This is a critically important analysis to make, for without a specific price range it may take an eternity to locate the right house. Review your budget to determine whether there are any unnecessary expenses that can be cut. What would you be willing to give up to buy this home? Entertainment? A new car? On the other hand, don't let your desire for your own home cause you to make unrealistic demands upon your family. For example, you may cut back on eating out, but don't expect to eat beans and peanut butter at home three meals a day, every day, for the next five years. Come to a reasonable decision about affordability prior to your house hunt.

Using an Agent Versus Looking for Yourself

The 1990s are definitely the years of the bargain shopper. Can you save money by eliminating the real estate agent? Yes, but it will cost you time. The issue is one of time and money — and which you have more of. If this is a first home purchase, chances are that money is an issue.

I have rarely used real estate agents in purchasing property. This is not to say that you should not, but the truly great bargains, in general, are not found in the offices of real estate agents. Most real estate investment strategists would agree.

The problem is that no matter how low a price appears to be, if a real estate agent is involved, so is a commission.

The only way to avoid having this commission built into the sales price is to seek out for-sale-by-owner properties, often listed as FSBO. This will limit the inventory for your choices, but if you are in a big market, that should not be a major problem.

If your situation allows you to pay a price that incorporates a commission of 5 to 8 percent, you may consider using an agent. If you do, be careful not to get "sold," but to find an agent who has your interests at heart. In almost all cases the agent will be representing the seller, not the buyer. So, as the adage states, "Let the buyer beware."

Let Your Fingers Do the Walking

Don't waste time visiting every property you read about in the newspaper or hear about from a friend. Earlier I said to research fifty to seventy-five properties — but only visit those properties that meet the criteria on your must list. This can be determined easily by telephone, if you ask the right questions. Here is an example of a typical conversation by an unseasoned shopper:

Buyer: "Hi, this is Mr. Jones. I'm calling about the ad you are running."

Seller: "Yes, how can I help you?"

Buyer: "Is the loan fully assumable without qualifying?"

Seller: "I don't really know for sure, but you can ask my husband if you would like to come out to see the house."

Buyer: "Great! Give me directions, and I'll see you tonight."

Notice a problem here? The buyer has not verified anything. He may waste an entire evening looking at a house that does not meet his requirements. The correct approach:

Buyer: "This is Mr. Smith, calling about your ad."
Seller: "Yes, how can I help you?"
Buyer: "Is the loan fully assumable, as stated in the ad?"
Seller: "Yes, it is."
Buyer: "Does the house have three bedrooms, two full baths and a screened-in porch?"
Seller: "Yes."
Buyer: "Is the property in a subdivision with a home owner's association?"
Seller: "Yes, it is."
Buyer: "Great! When may I come out to look at your home?"

The difference is that the second buyer has been thorough, not timid and agreeable. Every seller believes that he has the ideal property. If you do not aggressively phone-qualify on certain basics, the result will be hours of wasted time looking at houses that do not meet your specifications.

The Walk-through

Visiting properties can be fun and exciting. Always keep an open mind. Don't worry about the negotiations yet — rather decide if this is a house you could live in. Other than the obvious, here are some other considerations:
 • Condition of the neighborhood
 • Schools
 • Property taxes
 • Environmental hazards (flooding, and so on)
Always use a home inspection service before signing a sales agreement, but you can do an initial review by just using common sense and being observant. For example,

look for:
- Paint cracks that could indicate structural problems;
- Discolorations on ceilings that could indicate roofing problems;
- Standing water in yards that could indicate drainage problems.

New Home or Existing Home?

In my opinion buying an existing property and sprucing it up is a far better value than going to a new development and having a new home built on vacant land. Construction costs for a new home are usually much higher than buying a pre-owned home. This is especially true when the real estate market is depressed, or what we call a buyer's market, when there are more people trying to sell homes than there are people looking to buy them.

Negotiating

A survey in Orlando discovered that the average residential property sold for about 5 percent less than the asking price. This seems to be the norm in other cities as well. A rule of thumb, therefore, is that the seller will be willing to settle for about 5 percent less than the asking price, perhaps more. Occasionally properties in a certain area or market climate will be in such demand that they will sell for more than the asking price, but this is the exception rather than the rule.

It also helps to know about the seller. A motivated seller is one who is going through a divorce, a job transfer, a bankruptcy or another major event. Or it could be a home that is being sold as part of an estate. Be a good listener, as you can sometimes glean through casual conversation the reason for the sale. If not, ask why the owners are selling.

I bought my current residence from a man who had the property on the market for about a year and a half. He was very frustrated, and I probably met him at the height of his frustration. Initially he had asked a much higher price, and finally he dropped his price to what I believe was his lowest possible level. He was a motivated, flexible seller, which enabled the negotiations to go very smoothly.

The Follow-up Letter

Once you have located the house you would like to buy, send an informal letter thanking the owner for the opportunity to visit and outlining some possible terms. Here is an example:

Dear Mr. Jones:

Thank you for taking the time to show my wife and me your home. Although we are currently looking at several homes, we would be interested in discussing your home further if the following terms are possible:

Purchase Price:	$85,000
Seller Financing:	$10,000 (five-year mortgage)
Balance:	$75,000 assumable mortgage

We could close in thirty days and will pay all closing costs.

I look forward to hearing from you if you are interested. If not, we wish you all the best in your selling process.

Best regards,
James L. Paris

I would not recommend bringing in an attorney until you have an agreement and are ready to negotiate. If an attorney is brought in to draw up a purchase agreement every time you find a possibility, it will simply be too costly. The alternative is the informal letter approach. When you receive calls on these letters, return to the property to negotiate the deal. If there is a meeting of the minds, take your notes to an attorney and let him structure your purchase agreement. This has proved very successful in my house hunting.

Credit

One Sunday afternoon after church I was riding with a friend and the subject of home ownership came up. "I wish it were possible for me," he said. I questioned him about his belief that he could not become a home owner. He pointed out the two most common myths today: the need for excellent credit and the need for a substantial down payment.

If you are applying for a mortgage through a financial institution, you do need impeccable credit. In my city many of the banks require that you live in the area three years or longer or they won't even consider you for a mortgage. But there are alternatives:

Seller Financing
Many sellers can finance the purchase personally. These people usually have the property paid off and are planning to invest the sale proceeds to receive income during retirement. They usually will move to a smaller home, assisted-living center or condominium. Sometimes the availability of seller financing will be advertised, but in most cases you must ask.

A seller of real estate would normally like to receive all

cash and require the buyer to get financing, but in many circumstances the seller simply wants to sell as quickly as possible. Remember, when considering the possibility of seller financing, it is imperative to discover what the sale proceeds will be used for. If the seller needs the cash for a business opportunity, down payment on the next home or so on, this approach will not work. However, if the seller plans to invest the money, you can suggest that he will get a greater rate of return (usually about 3 to 5 percent better) by giving you a mortgage than by investing the money in bank CDs or other investment instruments. This is not a bad risk for the seller because, in the case of default, the seller can put the house back on the market and sell it again.

Assumable Financing

The second alternative to bank financing is assumable mortgages from the Veterans Administration (VA) and the Federal Housing Administration (FHA). You do not need to be a veteran to assume a VA loan, and you never need to visit an FHA loan office to assume an FHA loan. These loans are available in two types — qualifying and non-qualifying.

Nonqualifying properties will be listed in the classifieds as "VA/FHA — NQ." The nonqualifying mortgages do not require any credit rating, and you can even be new on the job. The buyer simply assumes the balance of the mortgage and pays closing costs, which vary from state to state. There is one problem, however, in that the seller may have built up equity in the property. Let's look at an example:

Sale Price	$85,000
Mortgage Balance	$75,000
Equity Balance	$10,000

If the buyer assumes payments on the $75,000 mortgage, he is still short $10,000 at closing time. The solution: Ask the seller to provide financing for the remaining $10,000 and assume the mortgage for $75,000, leaving only closing costs to be paid — this is how I purchased my second home. In this transaction no credit check or employment check was done. It was all based on my decision to buy.

Lease Option — Rent to Own

This is the third creative financing option, and it works well for someone who has bad credit. Let's say that you find a property selling for $100,000. The mortgage payment is $1,000 per month. Try to discover if the owner is a motivated seller. If so, you can suggest that you lease the property at $1,000 per month for three years. During that three-year period, the owner is to apply part of your rent payment toward a down payment so that you will be able to qualify for financing. You negotiate a sale price now so that you will be buying a property in three years at today's price, which is a plus for you because real estate generally appreciates in value.

Your attorney can draw up this agreement very easily. The seller is happy because he has your rental income to pay the mortgage on the property. And if after three years you decide not to buy the property, he keeps the accumulated principal credit, which he has applied to the property's purchase price.

It is not unusual to have 40 to 50 percent of the rent payment applied to your principal credit. Going back to our example, you have negotiated to buy a home for $100,000 in three years. You are going to lease the property for $1,000 per month and negotiate that $500 of the $1,000 payment will be applied as a principal credit toward the purchase of the property. In three years you will have a principal down payment or credit of $18,000 (half of the thirty-six $1,000 payments you have made). However, the home is now probably worth about $110,000 to $115,000, but you locked the price at $100,000 three years earlier. This leaves you with a mortgage of $82,000, which will equate to about an $825 monthly payment rather than $1,000. This is a fantastic strategy.

Conventional Financing

If you have good credit you may find a better deal with a new loan rather than assuming an existing one. I strongly recommend using a mortgage broker, who can search nationwide for the best interest rate and terms for your situation. A bank finance representative will have access only to his financial institution, which may not have the best available interest rates. A useful strategy is to inquire with two or three mortgage brokers and see who comes up with the best loan. Competition can be beneficial.

Two Basic Types of Loans

Fixed-Rate Mortgages

Fixed-rate mortgages offer the comfort factor of the same payment for the life of the loan. Are you the type of person who likes the consistency of knowing that your payment will be the same month after month, year after year? If so, this is your program.

Adjustable-Rate Mortgages

Adjustable-rate mortgages offer a rate lower than fixed rates, with the risk of that rate fluctuating during the life of the loan. Of course, if rates are high when you buy, you could benefit over the years because your ARM would be adjusted lower. On the other hand, a high fixed-rate loan can be refinanced, as has been the case with the unusually low rates that came in during the early 1990s.

My favorite mortgage variation is an adjustable rate with a conversion option. One bank in my area offered an ARM with a $100 conversion fee at any time during the first five years of the loan, which is quite attractive. A loan officer at your bank can explain to you other variations they have available on mortgage instruments.

ARMs are not as terribly risky as they might seem. They usually have caps — that is, a limit on the amount the interest rate can increase during the life of the loan and maximum yearly rate increases or decreases.

Fifteen- Versus Thirty-Year Mortgages

Most home buyers are amazed to learn that payments on a fifteen-year mortgage are not much more than on a thirty-year mortgage.

Example:

> $100,000 loan
> 9.5 percent interest rate
> Thirty-year payment = $840.86
> Fifteen-year payment = $1,044.23

Most buyers mistakenly assume that if the payment period is half the time, the payment must be twice as much, which is not true. The difference, of course, is in the amount of interest you pay over the life of the loan. Because of the way interest compounds, a thirty-year mortgage will cost you thousands of dollars more in interest that you could escape by paying in fifteen years.

For that reason, a fifteen-year mortgage can be an excellent "forced savings" program relative to the luxury of a thirty-year mortgage. The thirty-year, however, offers maximum flexibility. Remember, you can always accelerate the payment schedule on the thirty-year mortgage and accomplish the same end result, paying off the home in fifteen years. The only problem is discipline — will you make extra principal payments, or do you need the forced savings plan? You decide.

Investment Real Estate

I'm sure you have seen late-night television real estate gurus talking about how you can become a millionaire by investing in real estate. People ask me if this is true, and I respond that, yes, you can make big money in real estate. However, these entrepreneurs exaggerate their claims and oversimplify the process — they tend to glamorize it, not properly explaining the challenges involved in owning investment property. Many of these glib teachers have been successfully sued for misleading the public because they never mentioned the downside of owning investment property.

For example, let's say that in the mid-1980s you bought $1 million in real estate in Houston, just before oil prices took a nosedive. You would probably have gone bankrupt because of the high vacancies and economic problems that came into that area. Even in a city with a stable economy, you could easily buy the wrong properties and end up taking a loss. It is foolish to take the risks of rental properties lightly.

Here is my rule of thumb: For every rental property you purchase, you should have six months of the mortgage payment for that property in reserve to cover either tenant vacancies or major repairs to the property.

One way to locate good deals on rental properties is through local banks. They have properties on which they have foreclosed and will usually sell these for the principal balance owed. Sometimes they are sold at auctions. Another source is the Resolution Trust Corporation, which seized insolvent savings and loan institutions and their holdings in recent years. They are selling all sorts of properties for which the thrift institutions had made risky loans. For further information you can call the Resolution Trust Corporation at (800) 431-0600; or contact the U.S. Department of Housing and Urban Development, 451 Seventh Street SW, Washington, DC 20410.

Rental real estate affords many tax deductions, but it is a venture into which you should put a great deal of thought before investing.

Final Thoughts

Always make your property purchase contingent upon a satisfactory inspection of the property by a certified property inspector. This will cost you several hundred dollars but will prevent expensive surprises, such as roof problems, leaks in the plumbing and so on. If a problem is discovered, you will have to negotiate further as to whether the seller will pay to fix the problem or how much the sales price should be lowered. Sometimes the sale will fall through, but you will be better off not having an unexpected problem that could cost hundreds or thousands of dollars to fix.

Title insurance is a must, and it is standard in most purchase agreements. This means you pay for a company to research and insure that the seller is the only party with a claim to your property and is therefore in a position to transfer ownership to you without risk of a legal problem down the road.

Always, always, always bring in an attorney to draw up the final contract and close the deal.

Make your mortgage payment on time. If it is due on the first of the month, pay it by the first in order to save interest charges. Most mortgage companies give you until the fifteenth of the month before they assess a late penalty; but realize that interest accrues daily on the principal balance, so you are not saving anything by holding your payment until the fifteenth. In the long run it will cost you extra to operate that way.

Summary

Create a must list for the property you will buy, including needs and wants as well as financing needs. Take the time to look at as many properties that fit all of your criteria as possible, negotiate a good deal and have the home inspected.

Home ownership is a big financial step and a rewarding one. Is it for everyone? No. But if you plan to live in the same community for three to five years or longer, it should definitely be considered.

Questions

Prepaying Mortgages

Question: I have a thirty-year mortgage. Should I pay it off in fifteen years or just make the regular monthly payment and pay it off over thirty years?

Answer: I believe in paying off a mortgage in fifteen versus thirty years, especially if you are a young buyer, because it allows you to have extra money to commit toward your retirement plan when you pay off the house in your mid-forties. Regardless of your age, early mortgage payment is a wise idea.

There is a relatively small difference in monthly payments for a fifteen-year plan as opposed to a thirty-year plan because the longer version requires thousands of dollars in extra interest.

Essentially there are two ways to prepay a mortgage. One is called the extra principal payment strategy. What this means is when you look at your amortization schedule, which you can receive from your bank, you will see that every month, especially in the first five to ten years of your loan, the majority of the money you are paying goes toward interest and only a small amount toward principal. For example, a client in my office recently reviewed his amortization schedule and learned that on a $1,000 payment, only about $75 was going to reduce the principal. The strategy for him was simple: Pay the $1,000 payment and pay an additional $75, which represented the next month's principal payment. By doing that, he was actually making two full payments.

Now keep in mind that as the years go by, the amount of interest you are paying reduces and the amount of principal increases. In order to make next month's principal payment in the first five to ten years of a loan, it may be a simple matter of adding between $75 to $150 per month to your payment. In the latter years of the loan it may be as dramatic as making a virtual double payment, or in this example, adding an additional $1,000. Unless your income rises steadily and dramatically over the life of the loan, you may have trouble keeping up.

The other way to prepay a thirty-year mortgage in fifteen years is to create a more even flow of payments. You can do this by running a payment schedule with a computer or by using a financial calculator to determine what the equivalent payment would be for a fifteen-year mortgage. Generally speaking, increasing your payment by about 25 percent will do it. Financial Boot Camp for Christians software can determine for you, based on your goals, what your monthly payment should be.

Biweekly Mortgages

Question: I have been approached by an individual who is selling a biweekly mortgage system for $495. Is this a good idea?

Answer: No. While the idea of prepaying your home mortgage is good, paying someone else to do this type of calculation and provide this service is not.

The pitch goes something like this: If you pay half your mortgage payment every two weeks, instead of once per month, you'll be able to save hundreds or thousands of dollars over the life of your loan. Let's say that your mortgage payment is $1,000. Rather than making that payment monthly, you would make two payments of $500, one payment each two-week period. Because each year has twenty-six two-week periods, a $500 payment each two-week period would equal thirteen full payments, or $13,000 per year. If you were making monthly payments, you would have paid $12,000 per year.

So why spend $495 for a fancy printout and a bank service that will provide you with a biweekly payment book? Instead, make the equivalent of one extra full payment on the calendar anniversary of your mortgage every year. The result will be the same as the biweekly mortgage concept and will save you all the hassle of these expensive programs.

Buying a Run-down Home

Question: I'm considering buying a home that needs some work. I'm quite handy and don't see this as a problem. Actually, I see it as a great opportunity to buy a property at a good discount. Should I do this?

Answer: Many investors have bought fixer-upper properties, or what are known as "handyman specials." They do some very light cosmetic work, such as repainting or landscaping, then resell them for a profit of $10,000 to $15,000. On the other hand, these same experts tell me that many novice investors will buy properties that are in drastic need of a new roof, that have structural problems, electrical problems, plumbing problems and such. They end up sinking thousands of dollars into the property and lose their potential for profit. As in any other investment, you need to know as much as you can about where you are sinking your money.

One solution is to hire a certified property inspector. These specialists can be hired for about $250 or less and can completely review a property. They will list all problems they find. If you don't have the time to hire the inspector before you negotiate the price, write your contract up and make the purchase contingent upon satisfactory inspection by a certified property inspector. Once the evaluation is complete, you would then have the option of canceling the contract if the evaluation exposes problems that you are not willing to deal with in buying that property.

Mortgage Shopping

Question: There are various options relating to interest rates, points and fees. How do I make sure that I'm getting the best deal on a mortgage?

Answer: I recommend using a mortgage broker, an individual who shops the market to find the best deal for you. When I plan to travel, I find it inconvenient to call all of the airlines to find the best deal for the trip. So I call my travel agent, who has that information at his fingertips and assures me that I'm getting the best rate and the most convenient flight. Similarly, mortgage brokers have relationships with as many as thirty to forty financial institutions throughout the country.

By going directly to a bank, you are working with individuals who have only one option — to sign you up for financing with that bank. I would prefer to work with someone who is in a position to shop the marketplace.

Be careful to find out if the person you're working with is truly a mortgage broker who has access to multiple financial institutions. Ask how many financial institutions the broker works with. As always, when choosing a professional, ask friends and relatives for recommendations. If you really want to create some competition, call up two mortgage brokers, let them each shop for you and then go with the best deal.

"Points" in a Home Sale

Question: Recently while I was refinancing my home, the issue of "points" was raised. What is a point? And is that expense negotiable?

Answer: Essentially, a point is equal to 1 percent of the amount of money you are borrowing. If your mortgage loan is for $100,000 with one point, that would mean that $1,000 would be added to your loan as an expense.

The more you pay in points, the more you can reduce your interest rate. So it makes sense to pay more points for a lesser interest rate if you plan to stay in the property for five years or longer. Conversely, pay fewer points and receive a higher interest rate if you know you will be staying only short term in the property.

Points and other expenses are negotiable. It amazes me that so many people go into banks and pay the going interest rate, points and other fees and never even consider negotiating with the bank, as they would with an automobile dealer. Well, it's not quite the same, but, yes, banks do negotiate. Banks compete, just like other businesses. It doesn't hurt to ask if the terms of the loan are negotiable. Many times you will be surprised at the reduction of expenses, and even a better interest rate.

Title Insurance

Question: What is title insurance? Is it important?

Answer: Yes, yes, yes! Imagine someone informing you six months after you buy a property that they have a judgment against your property for $30,000. This does happen. As they relate to real estate, judgments are typically against the property and not the individual who owns it. Thus, if you buy a property with a judgment or lien against it, you are stuck with the payment of that lien.

The only way to avoid this is by transferring this risk to an insurance company. For a few hundred dollars when you purchase your property, you can obtain insurance known as title insurance. Title insurance insures that the property you are purchasing is free and clear from any judgment or liens. If judgments or liens are later found, the insurance company, not you, will have to pay those liens and judgments.

ELEVEN

THE LAND MINE
OF BANKRUPTCY

The wicked borrow and do not repay.
Psalm 37:21

Proverbs 22:7 (RSV) says, "The borrower is the slave of the lender." This has been true in societies throughout world history. In eighteenth-century England, as an alternative to being sentenced to debtor's prison, individuals were given the option of bankruptcy. Imagine going to prison for not being able to pay your debts! In 1841 the first major bankruptcy laws were passed in the United States. Before this legislation, imprisonment for not paying debts was commonplace.

Bankruptcy is now less publicly humiliating for the debtor but still nothing to take lightly. There are two basic forms of personal bankruptcy, known legally as Chapter 7 and Chapter 13.

Chapter 7 — Discharging of Debts

This form of bankruptcy should probably *not* be used by Christians unless the circumstances are entirely hopeless for debt repayment. Call me an extremist, but I believe the Bible is clear on this issue: We are to pay back money we have borrowed. After making what might be perceived as a legalistic comment, let me add that I don't think it is possible for everyone to repay their debts. Matthew 18:21-28 says:

> Then Peter came to Jesus and asked, "Lord, how many times shall I forgive my brother when he sins against me? Up to seven times?" Jesus answered, "I tell you, not seven times, but seventy-seven times. Therefore the kingdom of heaven is like a king who wanted to settle accounts with his servants. As he began the settlement, a man who owed him ten thousand talents was brought to him. Since he was not able to pay, the master ordered that he and his wife and his children and all that he had be sold to repay the debt. The servant fell on his knees before him. 'Be patient with me,' he begged, 'and I will pay back everything.' The servant's master took pity on him, canceled the debt and let him go."

If I understand the character of Jesus in this passage, I don't believe a person who *cannot* repay debts — as opposed to someone *unwilling* to repay — should be written off as a wicked person. The concept being taught in Psalm 37:21 is, in my opinion, dealing with improper attitudes about debt repayment. Believe it or not, there are people who borrow money with no intention of ever paying it back. There are also others who initially planned to repay the debt and later decided not to.

As a Christian financial educator I have heard a variety of creative justifications for refusing to repay a debt. One such perspective on this topic came from a woman who called me from Houston. The real estate market had dropped substantially in Houston, she said, and many of her neighbors were "walking away" from their houses. Indeed, many homes in Houston in the mid- to late 1980s were worth less than the outstanding mortgage, in some cases 50 percent less. These home owners were in a situation known as being "upside down" in their houses. Although this is a common phenomenon with automobiles, it rarely happens with a house.

According to this woman the commonly accepted solution was to let the property go into foreclosure and "let the bank deal with it." This cavalier attitude may sound harmless to you, but it is no different from what happened on a scale large enough to cause much of the savings and loan crisis. This attitude of leaving the problem to someone else is dangerous because eventually the burden falls to the government. Then you and I, the taxpayers, end up footing a bill that isn't supposed to be ours.

Chapter 13 — Bankruptcy

This is essentially a reorganization of the terms of an individual's debts. The intent behind Chapter 13 bankruptcy is to repay all creditors, albeit under more extended terms.

Once you file for Chapter 13 bankruptcy, all legal action against you related to your debts must stop. Furthermore, wage garnishments cannot be made against you. All creditors are prohibited from harassing you by letter, phone or in person. Generally they are required to work through your attorney.

Once you file for Chapter 13, a plan describing your proposed repayment schedule must be submitted to the court for approval. Once a plan is approved, your bankruptcy will be finalized. Such plans typically allow three to five years for repayment of debts.

As a Christian I feel that if bankruptcy is your only option, Chapter 13 is preferable to Chapter 7. Only in extreme circumstances, where repayment is not possible, should Chapter 7 be used.

Exempt Items From Bankruptcy

After filing for bankruptcy you will not be asked to relinquish all your earthly belongings and become a homeless person. Federal law allows for exempt items that can be retained after a bankruptcy. In addition, some states have laws that allow for even more property to be retained by the individual. These items are generally exempted:

• Your home.
• One motor vehicle with fair market value (FMV) of $1,200 or less.
• Household/personal property, FMV $4,000 or less.
• Insurance cash values.
• Tools of trade, FMV $750 or less.
• Future income from Social Security, corporate retirement plans, annuities and other exempt sources.

Harassment From Creditors

According to the Fair Debt Collection Practices Act, creditors are not allowed to cross the line of harassment. Creditors cannot:

• Contact you before 8 A.M. or after 9 P.M.
• Call you at work after you have notified them not to.

• Threaten you with arrest or any other scare tactics.

• Practice general harassment, such as contact friends, relatives, neighbors or coworkers about your debt.

If you feel your rights are being violated under the Fair Credit Debt Collection Practices Act, you may file a complaint with the Federal Trade Commission.

I would highly recommend locating a Christian bankruptcy attorney to assist you with the decision of whether or not to file bankruptcy and which form (Chapter 7 or 13) to employ. Most individuals who file for bankruptcy have not sincerely attempted to negotiate with their creditors. Most, but not all, creditors will try to work with you and will not force you into bankruptcy. In many cases a good bankruptcy attorney can act as a liaison with your creditors to assist you in avoiding bankruptcy.

Summary

Although many people have taken the position that bankruptcy is unscriptural, I don't agree, especially regarding Chapter 13 bankruptcy, which has a clear intent of debt repayment. I am not encouraging bankruptcy but simply explaining it. Some may choose to ignore this subject because it is controversial, but it is a reality for many Christians. And lest we forget one obvious Christian perspective on debt, consider this excerpt from the Lord's prayer: "And forgive us our debts, as we forgive our debtors" (Matt. 6:12, KJV).

For further information on bankruptcy procedures and fees, contact:

Administrative Office of the United States Courts
Bankruptcy Division
Washington, D.C. 20544
(202) 633-6231

TWELVE

THE LAND MINE OF DIVORCE

A righteous man may have many troubles,
but the Lord delivers him from them all.
Psalm 34:19

Needless to say, the breakup of the family is without a doubt one of the greatest destructive forces in our society. Christian counselors are reporting divorce rates as high as 50 percent of the number of new marriages — among Christians and non-Christians alike. Money is typically the leading issue that undermines these marriages.

Jesus said in Matthew 5:32, "But I tell you that anyone who divorces his wife, except for marital unfaithfulness, causes her to commit adultery, and anyone who marries a woman so divorced commits adultery." Yet many Christians view divorce as just another life option.

I am not a marriage counselor and have never been personally affected by divorce, either in my family or that of my parents. Yet as a financial counselor I am well aware of the financial side of divorce. I want to answer the question: How can you financially survive before, during and after a divorce? In no way am I advocating divorce, but the reality is that divorces are taking place at a record pace in the Christian community. For those who find themselves in this tragic circumstance, I highly recommend using a Christian attorney who specializes in family law. Contact your church and/or local bar association for referrals.

Before and After

I believe most marital differences can be resolved through prayer and counseling; but when it becomes evident that the marriage will not be salvaged, there are several areas of consideration.

Prenuptial Agreements

These premarriage financial contracts have grown in popularity over the past decade. They are not, however, a good way to start a marriage. While some financial advisers would recommend these arrangements as a protective measure in the event of divorce, the entire concept goes against the biblical principle of marriage. Matthew 19:5-6 says, "For this reason a man will leave his father and mother and be united to his wife, and the two will become one flesh...So they are no longer two, but one." Christian marriage should mean "our money," not "your money" and "my money." It should mean mutual self-sacrifice, not "my rights" and "your rights."

Credit

All too often I receive this call to my radio program, "Jim, I have ruined my credit...It's because of a divorce." Apparently one spouse decides that since the marriage is dissolving, it would be a great time to go on a spending spree. I have heard of individuals spending tens of thousands of dollars in two or three weeks on credit cards and other lines of credit. It must be some twisted form of revenge.

Remember, since most credit cards and credit lines are set up as joint accounts, either spouse can spend, but both share equally in the liability for repayment. Victims of a spouse's spending binge usually respond that it isn't fair. Maybe not, but it is the law. Thus this debt is now the responsibility of both individuals, and if not paid back on a timely basis, it will cause irreparable damage to their credit history.

There is a solution. Call your credit card companies, banks and other financial institutions and cancel all lines of credit over the phone immediately after you are aware of the impending divorce. Follow up with a certified letter *with a return receipt requested* (any post office will know how to do this). The letter should include:

• A statement that you will not be liable for any future transactions on the account as of the date of the letter.

• A request for information on how you can establish your own account(s).

You are legally responsible for any debts incurred *before* the notification — your letter is intended to close these accounts regarding *new* transactions. After the letter has been received, your lenders may decide to keep the accounts open. If so, you have legally protected yourself from the liabilities incurred after your letter.

Payments

The two most common issues in divorce settlements are:

• *Alimony*. These payments are deductible for the spouse paying them but are taxable income to the spouse receiving them.

• *Child support.* These payments are not deductible for the paying spouse or treated as income to the spouse receiving on behalf of children.

Because alimony is taxable and child support is not, it is to your advantage to structure your divorce settlement accordingly. For example, if you are the breadwinner of the family, you will most likely be making payments of support to your family as a result of the divorce settlement. The more of your income you can structure as alimony, the better, because it will be tax deductible. I am not encouraging dishonest tactics during negotiations but simply pointing out the legal strategies that are used.

The best result is a "win-win," where both parties are fairly dealt with. The nonworking or lower-wage-earning spouse should be aware that his or her spouse's attorney will most likely attempt to structure the settlement in the most tax-advantageous fashion for his client, which automatically creates a tax liability for the nonworking spouse.

Commerce Clearing House has produced a sixty-four-page booklet titled *Divorce and Taxes.* Among other things, it deals with how to structure alimony and child support so that both parties get the best financial results. Copies are available for $5 by writing or calling:

Commerce Clearing House, Inc.
Cash Item Department
4025 W. Peterson Ave.
Chicago, IL 60646
(800) 248-3248

Help With Child Support

We have all heard about the "deadbeat dads." These irresponsible individuals (many of whom profess to be Christians) have been able to skirt the authorities and avoid payments. Those days are coming to an end as many states have created child support enforcement offices to catch up with these men (or women) and make them pay.

The child support enforcement office can help you collect your money through the following actions:

• Wage garnishment.

• Credit bureau notification (which will ruin his or her credit).

• Income tax refunds withheld.

There are organizations in each state that can also save you thousands of dollars on legal fees by providing low-cost mediation and arbitration. Consult appendix H for an alphabetical listing by state.

Summary

Divorce is a wrenching emotional tragedy for both partners. But do not let the emotional trauma distract you from the practical matters you must quickly attend to regarding your credit. Get good legal counsel from the start to obtain the most fair, tax-wise settlement.

While negligence in child support and alimony is a sensitive matter, I do not want to paint with a broad brush and say that men — or for that matter, women — are most at fault for divorce. For all divorced Christians, a great verse to keep in mind while dealing with your former spouse is Ephesians 4:32 (NKJV): "And be kind to one another, tenderhearted, forgiving one another, even as God in Christ forgave you."

THIRTEEN

THE LAND MINE
OF UNWISE GIVING

*Jesus said, "I tell you the truth, this poor widow has
put more into the treasury than all the others. They all
gave out of their wealth; but she, out of her poverty,
put in everything — all she had to live on."*
Mark 12:43-44

I am deeply disturbed to hear of charities, both religious
and secular, that have taken people's last dimes, spent
the money unscrupulously without accomplishing their
missions and enriched the life-styles of their leaders
instead. Some of those most recently accused include the
PTL ministry, Mothers Against Drunk Driving, the Robert
Tilton television ministry and even United Way.

On the other hand, the Bible speaks about tithing, bringing gifts into the storehouse and assisting the poor, the hungry, the orphans and the widows. Malachi 3:10 says,
"'Bring the whole tithe [tenth] into the storehouse, that
there may be food in my house...,' says the Lord
Almighty." So we know that we are to give; the challenge
is to do so with wisdom. My desire in this chapter is to
mold you into wise givers.

167

Jesus spoke a parable about the final judgment in Matthew 25:31-46:

> When the Son of Man comes in his glory, and all the angels with him, he will sit on his throne in heavenly glory. All the nations will be gathered before him, and he will separate the people one from another as a shepherd separates the sheep from the goats. He will put the sheep on his right and the goats on his left.
>
> Then the King will say to those on his right, "Come, you who are blessed by my father; take your inheritance, the kingdom prepared for you since the creation of the world. For I was hungry and you gave me something to eat, I was thirsty and you gave me something to drink, I was a stranger and you invited me in, I needed clothes and you clothed me, I was sick and you looked after me, I was in prison and you came to visit me."
>
> Then the righteous will answer him, "Lord, when did we see you hungry and feed you, or thirsty and give you something to drink? When did we see you a stranger and invite you in, or needing clothes and clothe you? When did we see you sick or in prison and go to visit you?"
>
> The King will reply, "I tell you the truth, whatever you did for one of the least of these brothers of mine, you did for me."
>
> Then he will say to those on his left, "Depart from me, you who are cursed, into the eternal fire prepared for the devil and his angels. For I was hungry and you gave me nothing to eat, I was thirsty and you gave me nothing to drink, I was a stranger and you did not invite me in, I

needed clothes and you did not clothe me, I was sick and in prison and you did not look after me."

They also will answer, "Lord, when did we see you hungry or thirsty or a stranger or needing clothes or sick or in prison, and did not help you?"

He will reply, "I tell you the truth, whatever you did not do for one of the least of these, you did not do for me."

Then they will go away to eternal punishment, but the righteous to eternal life.

In my opinion the Bible does not necessarily teach that we must give the entire tenth of our income only to the church we attend. Some pastors feel that giving your complete tithe to the local church is scriptural and any giving beyond that represents offerings, which can go to organizations outside the church. My own conviction is to spread my contributions to secular and religious organizations I feel are doing good work. This, of course, includes the church I attend.

While the tithe — defined as 10 percent — is an Old Testament concept, the New Testament speaks broadly about giving generously. God allowed the Israelites to keep 90 percent of their income, minus certain offerings, whereas the New Testament teaches that *everything* we own and earn belongs to God. Acts 2:45, speaking of the early Christians, said, "Selling their possessions and goods, they gave to anyone as he had need."

Jesus instructs us to give to the poor, and I believe that we are to give as the Lord leads. Maybe He will urge you to give 30 percent or 50 percent of your income to charities and needy people. Perhaps you can provide some financial assistance to an ailing family member with the money you have set aside for giving. My wife has been known to arrive on people's doorsteps with grocery bags full of food when she learns of families who are struggling financially.

I feel that it is wise to set a pattern for giving and to meet needs as you see them. Holding fast to a strict 10 percent level is legalistic and precludes the Lord from working through you on behalf of others. Keep an open mind to the Lord as He leads you to where the funds would be of greatest use. Of course, I do believe that some of those funds should go to your home church, which performs a valuable service in your spiritual life. At the same time, however, there are missions works, both local and foreign, as well as many secular groups that meet basic needs outlined in the Bible.

Your Motive in Giving

I object to preachers who take Jesus' statement in Luke 6:38 out of context. The verse says, "Give and it will be given to you. A good measure, pressed down, shaken together and running over, will be poured into your lap." Some preachers insist that if you give to their ministries, God will pour great riches into your lap in return. This concept is also known as seed-faith giving.

The first problem with this interpretation is one of motives. We should never give to get. In Acts 20:35, our Lord is quoted as saying, "It is more blessed to give than to receive." God is not the Great Slot Machine in the Sky, who showers you with money when you put a coin into a ministry. Preachers who try to get your money by promising riches from God are appealing to greed. They should be calling you up to Christ, not calling you down to earthly possessions.

I am not saying God never blesses us, nor am I contradicting the scriptural principle that we reap what we sow.

But if God is the author of the good things we reap, the actual blessing and the timing of it are in His hands. For example, you may receive a blessing in ways other than material goods. Just because you send $1,000 to a ministry does not mean that the Lord will grant you your wishes for a new car or good health. You may not receive anything on earth for your good works and giving, but you will be rewarded in heaven. When you hear someone urging you to give so that you will receive, hold onto your wallet and run!

Know Your Recipients

In order to make sure your money is going to its proper use, you should give *more* than money; you should give your time as well, according to one of the top officials in the National Charities Information Bureau [(212) 929-6300]. Many charitable organizations need people for their day-to-day operations. Volunteering also allows you to get to know the people who are running an organization and to learn their true motives. Most of us have little time to spare, but even if it is just half a day per month, it could be time well spent — both for the organization and for you, as a wise giver.

Of course, many national or international organizations have no tasks you can help with on the local level. Still, you can use the following strategies to make sure you are wise in sending them your money.

• For giving to Christian organizations, especially para-church groups (those outside the church arena), I recommend contacting the Evangelical Council for Financial Accountability (ECFA) at (800) 323-9473 to find out whether an organization is a member. ECFA members must meet strict guidelines, including financial accountability and shared power within the organization.

If the organization you are interested in contributing to is not a member of ECFA, this does *not* automatically mean that it is an unscrupulous ministry. However, before giving money, I would inquire as to why the group is not a member.

• You can also check out certain Christian ministries, particularly those that use broadcast media, through the Ethics and Financial Integrity Commission (EFICOM). This organization is connected with National Religious Broadcasters, but it can also be reached through ECFA at (800) 323-9473.

• Another fundamental principle when giving to charities is to ask for a financial statement. If an organization is unwilling to provide you with this document, showing income and how the money was spent, including overhead expenses, compensation of executives, advertising expenses and so on, then I would *not* give a dime. Believe it or not, some very large and well-known charities have been guilty of spending 90 percent of their income on the salaries and administrative overhead! That means that less than 10 percent of your gift actually goes to the cause they espouse. Refusal to disclose the facts and figures should be a red flag that you are about to enter a mine field.

• If a financial statement is unavailable from the charity, you may consider contacting the Internal Revenue Service. The IRS keeps the tax returns of nonprofit organizations on file for the general public's scrutiny. To obtain one, you would call (800) 829-1040 to get the phone number and address of the IRS disclosure officer for your area. There will be a fee for the information. Tax returns can be helpful but not as clear as a financial statement, which should be available quarterly from charities.

• Prayer should be part of determining your giving. Investing in people is more valuable than storing up treasures on this earth, where, as Jesus said, moth and rust decay. Even though you won't get a tax deduction for giving to individuals, the Bible states that rewards are waiting for those who do the Father's will, which includes helping those around us. Ask in prayer for direction, and the Holy Spirit will guide you to the right charities and people who are in need.

For example, a friend was convinced that the Lord was telling her to give $2,000 to a couple she knew. She purchased a greeting card and enclosed the money, handing it to the couple without a word of explanation.

Later she learned this couple had a very specific and urgent need for $2,000, and they were very grateful. Through this gift she enabled the Lord to be glorified in her life as well as in this family.

Summary

Giving is an essential part of the Christian experience. Even though you hear of financial abuse in some organizations, don't allow a few bad apples to spoil the whole barrel. The answer is not to stop giving, but to start giving *wisely*. Obtain a financial statement from the organization, recognizing that a group's refusal to furnish one should alert you to avoid them. Give of your time as well as your money in order to see firsthand how well the organization operates. And, finally, commit your giving to prayer so that the Lord has an opportunity to reveal needs you may be able to meet.

FOURTEEN

The Land Mine
of Poor Tax
Planning

*"Give to Caesar what is Caesar's
and to God what is God's."
Mark 12:17*

A friend was excited about his new job. One reason was that part of his compensation was going to be in cash, from tips. I asked him why this was so great. He responded that he didn't plan to report tips to the Internal Revenue Service, so he would be able to keep more of his income.

I challenged him on the ethics of this response, especially because this individual is a Christian. He said the government wastes too much of its tax revenue, that the IRS is an unfair organization and that as long as the government was unaware of his extra income, no one would be hurt.

The Bible is very clear about Christians and taxes. Mark 12:13-17 tells about the Pharisees trying to trap Jesus Christ into saying that taxes shouldn't be paid. Jesus asked

174

for a coin, and then He asked them whose picture appeared on the coin. They responded, "Caesar's," the leader of the Roman Empire. Jesus then said, "Give to Caesar what is Caesar's." In other words, we have a responsibility to pay our share of taxes.

In Romans 1 Paul says God is the One who puts governments in power and that civil government serves a clear purpose to maintain law and order. We must obey governmental leadership and civil law, including the payment of taxes, provided the government does not command us to break God's laws, which are our higher calling.

One of the Ten Commandments prohibits lying, or bearing false witness against a neighbor. I believe that false witness of any kind is abhorrent to God. If a person files a tax return that does not disclose all income or includes false information about deductions, this is nothing more than lying.

Trying to twist tax laws to fit your situation is unethical and not pleasing to God. However, there is nothing wrong with a Christian having a tax plan. We can obey tax laws while using them to our advantage. That is the focus of this chapter.

Itemizing and Record Keeping

Circuit Judge Learned Hand said, "Anyone may so arrange his affairs that his taxes shall be as low as possible. He is not bound to choose a pattern that will best pay the Treasury." So even the government recognizes that there is nothing illegal about structuring your financial affairs in order to pay lower taxes.

To do so, the first basic concept is itemizing deductions. If you are not currently taking advantage of itemizing your deductions on Schedule A of the federal income tax, start doing so. If you are not doing so, then you are taking the standard deduction and thereby paying the highest tax possible to the IRS each year.

Itemizing deductions takes planning and organizing. To complete Schedule A, you need to have figures from your medical bills, property and local tax bills, interest payments on mortgages and charitable contributions. But it is worth the effort. These expenses will usually add up to thousands of dollars more than the standard deduction, especially if you have a moderate or large home mortgage.

It is very difficult and frustrating for me to sit down with a client seeking tax help and to have him look blankly at me when I ask to see his record keeping for the past year. This task is so simple, yet so few of us have the discipline to keep our records in order so we can be good stewards of our taxable income.

How do you start? Set up file folders at the beginning of each year for each regular bill that you pay. Discipline yourself to use these files, and at the end of the year most of your work will have been done for you. To help your record keeping, pay for as many bills and charitable gifts as possible by check. Those cancelled checks and your checking record serve as an accounting system.

Taxpayers need to become familiar with tax laws and any new legislation that relates to personal income taxes in order to use the tax laws to their advantage. The IRS provides hundreds of free publications on everything from preparing your own tax return to small business deductions. You can obtain these by calling (800) 829-1040.

Second, there are many books written every year on the subject of taxes. I would recommend the *Guide to Income Tax Preparation* by the Consumer Reports company as well as *J.K. Lasser's Guide to Income Tax Preparation*. I read the updated versions of these publications each year.

If you don't already do so, take the time next year to prepare your own taxes. Not only will you save the sometimes-hefty preparation fees, but your eyes will be opened to the many deductions and exemptions you may qualify for. I have been preparing my own taxes for years, and it is not difficult. The tax laws are very complicated, but once you learn how the IRS thinks, it becomes very easy to interpret the tax law. There is a pattern to the tax laws, and the trends are easy to learn.

If you have a personal computer, a number of software programs can help you prepare your own tax returns. I use a popular program called Turbo Tax, made by ChipSoft.

Once you begin to prepare your own tax return, you will find yourself thinking throughout the year about ways to take advantage of deductions. For example, a new baby born during the year will provide a tax exemption (not that you can always count on its arriving before January 1!). The IRS allows tax deductions for employee mileage expenses that are not reimbursed by your employer, though you must keep a travel log to prove the expense. Child care expenses related to a parent's work can be deducted.

One of the obvious strategies that comes from familiarity with the tax code involves timing. For example, you may be planning to make large, tax-deductible expenditures — such as a charitable contribution or an investment in a small business you have — in the early months of next year. It would be better to move those expenditures up into December so that you can deduct them the next April, instead of having to wait until April of the following year.

Qualified Retirement Plans

There are a variety of qualified retirement plans available to you. Some of the names that may be familiar to you are 401(k), 403(b), deferred compensation plans and profit-sharing plans. These are excellent opportunities for a wage-earner to put away hundreds of thousands of dollars over his or her lifetime. Some of the employer-matching plans discussed in chapter 6 on retirement planning are 401(k) plans.

Rather than paying taxes on the money put into these plans at the time it is earned, monies are contributed tax-deferred, meaning that income taxes will not be paid until the money is withdrawn from the retirement plan. It is always good to save, but here you get the added benefit of skipping taxes for years on the money you use for savings, as well as on the earnings that accumulate from your savings.

One little-known tax strategy is that the IRS will allow a person who has his own small business to set up a self-employed pension individual retirement account (SEP IRA). The small business owner can put away up to $30,000 per year, not to exceed 15 percent of his adjusted gross income, tax-deferred. That is a tremendous benefit. I have set these plans up for doctors, lawyers and many other clients. If you are a small business owner, you should seriously consider this tax-saving benefit.

Allowances and the W-4 Form

Many people like a big refund from the IRS at tax time. It's as if they think the IRS is giving them a gift. Nothing could be further from the truth! You need to be taking home as much of your paycheck as possible. This will mean no springtime Christmas present from Uncle Sam, but that's OK.

Your refund is based on the number of allowances you claim on the W-4 form you fill out when you start a new job. By claiming zero or one allowance, you are asking the employer to withhold the maximum amount possible. Usually this amount will be far greater than the taxes you will owe; hence your annual refund.

The problem with this is you are giving the government an interest-free loan for a full year. Wouldn't it be a better idea for you to have that money to invest and gain interest for you, rather than allowing the government to use it?

You need to change your thinking. Getting a large refund in April means that you did not manage your resources properly. Go to your employer's personnel department and request a new W-4 form. Increase the number of allowances you claim. If you have three dependents, you should be claiming at least four (counting yourself) on your W-4.

The federal withholding from your wages will decrease, so your paycheck will increase. Place this extra money into a good investment, like a no-load mutual fund, where it will gain interest. Your money will be worth *more* the following April than if you had received it back from the government, because interest will have accumulated *in your favor*.

Individual Retirement Accounts

Individual retirement accounts can be set up using many types of investments. In some cases the new money you place in an IRA each year is tax deductible, and all the interest on that money grows tax-deferred. I believe that all adults should take advantage of these accounts, whether they are employed or not. Our government has allowed us to accumulate money tax-deferred, and it is an option that should not be overlooked. You can invest your IRA in any of the mutual funds we have discussed in a previous chapter, such as Twentieth Century, Fidelity, the Financial Funds and so on.

If neither you nor your spouse has access to a qualified retirement plan through your employers, then regardless of your income you have access to a fully tax-deductible $2,000 investment in an IRA each year. For a nonworking

179

spouse the amount drops to $250 fully tax-deductible. If you do have access to a qualified retirement plan through your employer, and you are single and make less than $25,000 per year, you qualify for the $2,000 fully tax-deductible IRA investment.

If you are married and filing jointly with a qualified plan from your employer, the maximum income jumps to $40,000 total for the fully deductible $2,000 investment. However, if your joint income totals more than $40,000, and one or both spouses have access to a qualified plan from an employer, there is no deductible investment allowed to an IRA.

Remember that IRA earnings grow tax-deferred, so even if your yearly IRA investments are not deductible, it still makes sense to have an IRA. IRAs provide two basic benefits: tax-deferred growth (in some cases, tax deduction), and funds for your retirement.

After you have placed the maximum allowable monies in your IRA and qualified employer plans each year, what should you do if you wish to invest further for your retirement? Consider a mutual fund annuity. These investments allow for unlimited contributions, and your money grows tax-deferred. Once in the annuity, you can choose any type of mutual fund available within the annuity. I believe that in the 1990s Congress will tighten the rules regarding annuities and will create maximum contribution levels for these as well. It would be wise to get one started now.

My favorite mutual fund annuity is called The Best of America, provided through Nationwide Insurance Company of Columbus, Ohio. This annuity features some of the best mutual funds in the country, including Twentieth Century, Newburger Berman, Fidelity and others. It has an impressive track record.

Summary

Arrange your investments to reduce your taxes as much as possible. Become an itemizer and keep good records throughout the year. Learn to prepare your own taxes so that you are aware of the tax deductions available to you. Structure your W-4 exemptions to allow you to pay the correct amount of tax withholding each paycheck, and invest that which you used to have withheld. Utilize IRAs to your maximum benefit, depending on your individual situation. Educate yourself! Order those free publications from the IRS, familiarize yourself with the current tax laws and trends, and keep abreast of the changes in the tax legislation.

There is no reason you cannot arrange your affairs to reduce your tax burden. Doing so is part of your stewardship of the resources given you by our Lord.

FIFTEEN

The Land Mine of Improper Estate Planning

Death is the destiny of every man.
Ecclesiastes 7:2

We all have one thing in common — we will die. We don't like to think about that very often, but at some point we need to make some important plans regarding the final chapter of our lives.

Imagine dying and having your assets distributed by someone else. In many states the state gets the job of distributing a person's assets because no will was left. Whom would you like to be the guardian of your minor children if something happened to you and your spouse? How much would you like to have the government receive in estate taxes?

Most people do not have a proper estate plan. If the issue doesn't seem important to you, I hope you will reconsider it as you read this chapter. Whatever your age, you are not too young to address these matters.

Wills

A will is the most basic document in estate planning. Here are some essentials about wills:

• *A will handles the proper distribution of assets.* Your intentions for your personal and real property will be accomplished by a will. This allows you to leave special bequests to people or organizations.

Some states require you to give a certain percentage of your assets to a surviving spouse and children. If this is the case state law will override anything to the contrary that may be in your will.

• *A will appoints a guardian for minor children.* This is very important because there are persons you would prefer for teaching your children the values you want them to have. If you do not spell out your wishes for guardianship, state law will determine who raises your minor children.

• *A will must go through probate.* Probate is the proving process. Through the court system, a judge decides whether the will is authentic, valid and legal in your state and whether it was written while you were mentally competent.

• *It takes time to settle the affairs in a will.* In many states the probate process can take as long as a year or more to be settled. At the writing of this book John Wayne's estate is still in probate, and he died in 1979. Marilyn Monroe's estate was in probate for almost eighteen years. Groucho Marx's estate went through probate three times. In California, probate now takes between two and three years.

• *A will in probate is a public document.* Anyone can go to the county courthouse and review the contents of a will that is going through probate. This is uncomfortable to some people because a will, by its very nature, divulges private information. Also, probate is a public proceeding, and anyone can be present during the process.

Often insurance salesmen and financial planners go to

the courthouse to check on wills. They are looking for leads on people who may be inheriting large amounts of money and who may be interested in their services.

• *Expenses of probate can be 10 percent or more of the estate.* Attorneys who take a will from start to finish are entitled to a percentage of the entire estate, and this is usually in the thousands of dollars.

• *A will does not protect you from conservatorship.* If you are declared mentally incompetent, meaning that you are judged unable to make certain basic decisions, especially financial ones, a court will be appointed to serve as conservator. All expenses incurred on your behalf must then be presented to the court, usually on a quarterly basis. It's a bookkeeping nightmare and something that everyone should want to avoid.

Dying without a will is called dying intestate. This is the worst situation because the state then decides who receives your assets and also who will be the guardian of any minor children you may have.

The quick answer to this is not to title your major assets with joint names, typically parent and child. This would produce legal problems in case of a divorce or lawsuits. If you title your house jointly with one of your children, a lawsuit against your child could bring your home into the lawsuit. The same could happen if your child goes through a divorce; your home would be part of the divorce settlement because, according to the courts, it's part of his assets.

Perhaps you decide that you will give your property and assets to your survivors prior to your death. You need to be careful with the value of the gifts you give because there are limits set by the government concerning gift-giving. Above those limits, you incur hefty taxes. The government clearly plans to penalize those who try to avoid estate and inheritance taxes by giving away big chunks of assets before their deaths.

Living Trusts

A living trust is a legal arrangement where one or more trustees manage property for a beneficiary or beneficiaries. I will talk about *revocable* living trusts. There are three basic benefits of a living trust:
- *They avoid the probate process.*
- *They avoid conservatorship.*
- *They save taxes.*

Many people believe that if they set up a revocable living trust, they will lose control of their assets. They assume that a bank or some outside person must be the trustee. This is false. You can be the manager of the trust and decide where the money will be invested and spent. You do not lose control when you set up a revocable living trust.

A revocable living trust can be changed or terminated — hence the term *revocable*. I don't recommend irrevocable trusts, though they have their place under some circumstances, which I will not discuss here.

Trusts are not only for the rich. They are primarily for individuals who have an estate worth at least $600,000, who wish to avoid probate and conservatorship, and who wish to save on estate taxes.

One of the biggest attractions of revocable living trusts is their tax savings. The federal government gives each individual or married couple a $600,000 exemption from taxes being charged against their estates upon their death. Any assets above that amount are subject to federal estate taxes.

With a revocable living trust, married couples can gain an extra $600,000 exemption through a unified credit strategy. This means that each spouse takes his or her exemption and combines it with the other spouse, giving a married couple $1.2 million of sheltered assets. This is called a his-and-hers trust plan or an A/B trust.

185

An attorney can design a revocable living trust for you. Although you will incur some expense when the trust is set up, it is far less than what your estate will be charged upon your death.

Summary

You need to have a will. It gives the proper distribution of your assets and appoints the correct guardian for any minor children.

If your estate is valued at more than $600,000, then the revocable living trust is for you. The trust avoids probate and conservatorship and saves money on estate taxes through the A/B trust.

Federal Trade Commission Regional Offices

Atlanta (AL, FL, GA, MS, NC, SC, TN, VA)
Federal Trade Commission
1718 Peachtree St. NW, Room 1000
Atlanta, GA 30367
(404) 881-4836

Boston (CT, ME, MA, NII, RI, VT)
Federal Trade Commission
150 Causeway St., Room 1301
Boston, MA 02114
(617) 223-6621

Chicago (IL, IN, IA, KY, MN, MO, WI)
Federal Trade Commission
55 E. Monroe St., Ste. 1437
Chicago, IL 60603
(312) 353-4423

Cleveland (DE, MD, MI, OH, PA, WV)
Federal Trade Commission
Mall Building, Ste. 500
118 St. Clair Ave.
Cleveland, OH 44114
(216) 522-4207

Dallas (AR, LA, NM, OK, TX)
Federal Trade Commission
8303 Elmbrook Dr.
Dallas, TX 75247
(214) 767-7050

Denver (CO, KS, MT, NE, ND, SD, UT, WY)
Federal Trade Commission
1405 Curtis St., Ste. 2900
Denver, CO 80202
(303) 844-2271

Los Angeles (AZ, Southern CA)
Federal Trade Commission
11000 Wilshire Blvd.
Los Angeles, CA 90024
(213) 824-7575

New York (NJ, NY)
Federal Trade Commission
Federal Bldg., Room 2243-EB
26 Federal Plaza
New York, NY 10278
(212) 264-1207

San Francisco (Northern CA, HI, NV)
Federal Trade Commission
450 Golden Gate Ave., Room 12470
San Francisco, CA 94102
(808) 546-5685
(206) 442-4655

Seattle (AL, ID, OR, WA)
Federal Trade Commission
Federal Bldg., 28th Floor
915 Second Ave.
Seattle, WA 98174
(206) 553-4655

State Attorney Generals' Offices

Alabama
11 S. Union St.
Montgomery, AL 36130
(205) 242-7300

Alaska
Department of Law
P.O. Box K
Juneau, AK 99811
(907) 465-3600

Arizona
1275 W. Washington
Phoenix, AZ 85007
(602) 542-4266

Arkansas
323 Center #200
Little Rock, AR 72201
(501) 682-2007

California
1515 K St. Law Library
Sacramento, CA 95814
(916) 324-5437

Colorado
1525 Sherman St., 3rd Floor
Denver, CO 80203
(303) 866-5005

Connecticut
55 Elm St.
Hartford, CT 06016
(203) 566-2026

Delaware
820 N. French St.
Wilmington, DE 19801
(302) 571-2500

Florida
The Capitol
Tallahassee, FL 32399
(904) 487-1963

Georgia
132 State Judicial Bldg.
Atlanta, GA 30334
(404) 656-4585

Hawaii
State Capitol
Honolulu, HI 96813
(808) 548-4740

Idaho
State Capitol
Boise, ID 83720
(208) 334-2400

Illinois
500 S. Second St.
Springfield, IL 62706
(217) 782-1090

Indiana
219 State House
Indianapolis, IN 46204
(317) 232-6201

Iowa
Hoover State Office Bldg.
Des Moines, IA 50319
(515) 281-8373

Kansas
Judicial Center
Topeka, KS 66612
(913) 296-2215

Kentucky
State Capitol, Room 116
Frankfort, KY 40601
(502) 564-7600

Louisiana
Department of Justice
P.O. Box 94005
Baton Rouge, LA 70804
(504) 342-7013

Maine
State House Station #6
Augusta, ME 04333
(207) 289-3661

Maryland
7 N. Calvert
Baltimore, MD 21202
(301) 576-6300

Massachusetts
1 Ashburton Pl.
Boston, MA 02108
(617) 727-3688

Michigan
525 W. Ottawa
Law Bldg.
Lansing, MI 48913
(517) 373-1110

Minnesota
102 State Capitol
St. Paul, MN 55155
(612) 297-4272

Mississippi
Gartin Bldg., 5th Floor
Jackson, MS 39201
(610) 359-3680

Missouri
P.O. Box 899
Jefferson City, MO 65102
(314) 751-3221

Montana
215 N. Sanders St.
Helena, MT 59620
(406) 444-2026

Nebraska
Capitol Complex
P.O. Box 94906
Lincoln, NE 68509
(402) 471-2682

Nevada
Room 2115, State Capitol
Carson City, NV 68509
(702) 885-4170

New Hampshire
208 State House Annex
235 Capitol St.
Concord, NH 03301
(603) 271-3658

New Jersey
Department of Law and
    Public Safety
25 Market St.
CN080
Trenton, NJ 08625
(609) 292-4976

New Mexico
Bataan Memorial Bldg.
P.O. Box 1508
Santa Fe, NM 87501
(505) 827-6000

New York
Department of Law
State Capitol
Albany, NY 12224
(518) 474-7330

North Carolina
Department of Justice
2 E. Morgan St.
Raleigh, NC 27601
(919) 733-3377

North Dakota
1st Floor, State Capitol
600 East Blvd.
Bismarck, ND 58505
(701) 224-2210

Ohio
30 E. Broad St., 17th Floor
Columbus, OH 43266
(614) 466-3376

Oklahoma
112 State Capitol
Oklahoma City, OK 73105
(405) 521-3921

Oregon
Department of Justice
100 State Office Bldg.
Salem, OR 97310
(503) 370-6002

Pennsylvania
Strawberry Square,
    16th Floor
Harrisburg, PA 17120
(717) 787-3391

Rhode Island
72 Pine St.
Providence, RI 02903
(401) 274-4400

South Carolina
Dennis Bldg.
P.O. Box 11549
Columbia, SC 29211
(803) 734-3970

South Dakota
1st Floor, State Capitol
Pierre, SD 57501
(605) 773-3215

Tennessee
450 James Robertson Pkwy.
Nashville, TN 37219
(615) 741-6474

Texas
Box 12548, Capitol Station
Austin, TX 78711
(512) 463-2100

Utah
236 State Capitol
Salt Lake City, UT 84114
(801) 538-1324

Vermont
Pavilion Office Bldg.
109 State St.
Montpelier, VT 05602
(802) 828-3171

Virginia
101 N. Eighth St., 5th Floor
Richmond, VA 23219
(804) 786-2071

Washington
Hwy. Licenses Bldg.
M/S:PB-71
Olympia, WA 98504
(206) 753-2550

West Virginia
State Capitol Complex
Bldg. 1, Room E-26
Charleston, WV 25305
(304) 348-2021

Wisconsin
114 E. State Capitol
P.O. Box 7857
Madison, WI 54707
(608) 266-1221

Wyoming
State Capitol
Cheyenne, WY 82002
(307) 777-7810

Credit Card Sources

Here are sources of credit cards which, at the time of the writing of this book, had the best rates and terms in the country. Though conditions change, these sources have historically been leaders in good credit terms.

Low-Interest-Rate Credit Cards (Variable Interest Rate)

Bank of Hawaii
Honolulu, HI
(808) 543-9611

Valley Bank
Las Vegas, NV
(702) 654-1165

First National of Omaha
Omaha, NE
(800) 688-7070

Wachovia Card Services
Newark, DE
(800) 842-3262

Simmons First National
Pine Bluff, AR
(501) 541-1304

Low-Interest-Rate Credit Cards (Fixed Interest Rate)

First United Bank
Bellevue, NE
(800) 635-8503

People's Bank
Bridgeport, CT
(800) 423-3273

National Bank of Alaska
Anchorage, AK
(907) 276-1132

Wachovia Bank
Salem, NC
(800) 241-7990

Ohio Savings
Cleveland, OH
(800) 354-1445

Low-Interest-Rate Gold Cards

Amalgamated Trust
Chicago, IL
(800) 365-6464

Simmons First National
Pine Bluff, AR
(501) 541-1304

Central Carolina Bank
Durham, NC
(919) 683-7777

Wachovia Card Services
Newark, DE
(800) 842-3262

National Bank of Alaska
Anchorage, AK
(907) 276-1132

Low-Interest-Rate, No-Annual-Fee Credit Cards

Community Bank of Parker
Parker, CO
(800) 779-8472

Union Planters National
Memphis, TN
(800) 628-8946

Fidelity National
Atlanta, GA
(800) 753-2900

USAA Federal Savings
San Antonio, TX
(800) 922-9092

Secured Credit Cards

American Pacific Bank
Portland, OR
(800) 879-8745

Dreyfus Thrift
Old Beth Page, NY
(800) 727-3348

Community Bank of Parker
Parker, CO
(800) 779-8472

First Consumers
Seattle, WA
(800) 876-3262

College/Occupational Reference Sources

The A's & B's of Academic Scholarships
by Debbie Klein
$6 plus $1.75 postage
Contact: Octameron Associates
             P.O. Box 2748
             Alexandria, VA 22301

CFKR Career Materials Catalog
Free
Contact: CFKR Career Materials, Inc.
             11860 Kemper Rd., Unit 7
             Auburn, CA 95603

College Board Guide to the CLEP Examinations
$11.95
Contact: College Board Publications
             P.O. Box 886
             New York, NY 10101

College Financial Aid Emergency Kit
by Joyce Kennedy and Dr. Herm Davis
$5.50
Contact: Sun Features, Inc.
             Box 368-K
             Cardiff, CA 92007

Directory of Educational Institutions
$5
Contact: Association of Independent Colleges
                 and Schools
             1 Dupont Circle #350
             Washington, DC 20036

Fiske Guide to Colleges
$15
Contact: New York Times Books
             400 Hahn Rd.
             Westminster, MD 21157

Making It Through College
$1
Contact: Professional Staff Congress
             25 W. 43rd St., 5th Floor
             New York, NY 10036

Need a Lift?
$2
Contact: American Legion Education Program
             P.O. Box 1050
             Indianapolis, IN 46206

Occupational Outlook Handbook
$17
Contact: Superintendent of Documents
             U.S. Government Printing Office
             Washington, DC 20402

Power Study to Up Your Grades and GPA
by Sondra Geoffrion
$3.95 plus $2.50 postage
Contact: Access Success Associates
            P.O. Box 1686
            Goleta, CA 93116

Student Guide to Financial Aid
Free
Contact: Federal Student Aid Information Center
            P.O. Box 84
            Washington, DC 20044

Ten Steps in Writing the Research Paper
by Robert Markman, Peter Markman and Marie Waddell
$7.95
Contact: Barron's Educational Series Inc.
            250 Wireless Blvd.
            Hauppauge, NY 11788

History of the Real Return of a Certificate of Deposit

Year	6-Month Rates*	Less Taxes†	Less Inflation	Real Return‡
1970	7.65%	50%	5.5%	-1.67%
1971	5.21%	50%	3.4%	-0.79%
1972	5.02%	50%	3.4%	-0.89%
1973	8.31%	50%	8.8%	-4.65%
1974	9.98%	62%	12.2%	-8.41%
1975	6.89%	62%	7.0%	-4.38%
1976	6.62%	62%	4.8%	-2.28%
1977	5.92%	60%	6.8%	-4.43%
1978	8.61%	60%	9.0%	-5.56%
1979	11.44%	59%	13.3%	-8.61%
1980	12.99%	59%	12.4%	-7.07%
1981	15.77%	59%	8.9%	-2.43%
1982	12.57%	50%	3.9%	2.39%
1983	9.27%	48%	3.8%	1.02%
1984	10.68%	45%	4.0%	1.87%
1985	8.25%	45%	3.8%	0.74%
1986	6.50%	45%	1.1%	2.48%
1987	7.01%	38%	4.4%	0.05%
1988	7.85%	33%	4.4%	0.86%
1989	9.08%	33%	4.6%	1.48%
1990	8.17%	31%	6.1%	-0.46%
1991	6.76%	31%	3.0%	1.66%
1992	3.44%	31%	3.2%	-0.83%

Source: Federal Reserve Board and Consumer Price Index

* Annualized average monthly rates

† I used the highest tax rate for a given year in order to illustrate my point clearly. If you are considering purchasing CDs, you can customize this chart for yourself. Simply apply your own tax rate to the CD yield and subtract the current inflation.

‡ After taxes and inflation

Top Twenty No-Load/Low-Load
Mutual Funds for 1981-1990

This list does not constitute a recommendation to purchase any particular mutual fund. In considering a purchase of these funds or any others, do not rely solely on historical performance, which is no guarantee of future results.

	Name of Fund	Annualized Rate of Return	
		Five Years	*Ten Years*
1.	Fidelity Magellan	14.5	21.2
2.	Japan (Scudder)	21.3	18.8
3.	CGM Capital Development	12.2	17.7
4.	Sequoia	10.5	17.5
5.	Quest for Value	8.0	17.3
6.	Lindner Dividend	8.5	17.0
7.	Mutual Qualified	11.0	16.5
8.	Lindner Fund	9.9	16.5
9.	Twentieth Century Fund	13.3	15.7
10.	Janus	14.4	15.7
11.	Windsor (Vanguard)	8.8	15.7
12.	T. Rowe Price (Int'l Stock Fund)	18.3	15.6
13.	1A1 Regional	15.0	15.5
14.	AIM Weingarten Equity	17.0	15.2
15.	Mutual Shares	11.0	15.2
16.	Century Shares Trust	8.8	15.1
17.	Financial Industrial Inc.	13.0	14.9
18.	Ivy Growth	9.6	14.9
19.	Nicholas Fund	9.2	14.9
20.	Endowments	11.9	14.8

No-Load and Low-Load Mutual Funds

These addresses and phone numbers will give you access to more than four hundred funds. You may request more detailed information about the fund's philosophies, holdings, performance and so on. Should a number no longer be in service, try dialing (800) 555-1212 to see if a toll-free number is in service.

AARP Funds
160 Federal St.
Boston, MA 02110
(800) 631-INFO

The Acorn Fund
2 N. LaSalle St.
Chicago, IL 60602
(800) 9-ACORN-9

Active Assets Government
  Security Trust
5 World Trade Center,
  6th Floor
New York, NY 10048
(800) 869-3326

Adam Investors Inc.
Wood Island, 4th Floor
80 E. Sir Francis Drake Blvd.
Larkspur, CA 94939
(415) 461-3850

Afuture Fund Inc.
617 Willowbrook Ln.
West Chester, PA 19382
(800) 523-7594

AIM Funds
11 Greenway Plaza,
  Ste. 1919
Houston, TX 77046
(800) 347-1919

Allegro Growth Fund Inc.
P.O. Box 74450
Cedar Rapids, IA 52407
(319) 366-8400

Alliance Funds
1345 Avenue of the Americas
New York, NY 10105
(800) 221-5672

Amana Income Fund
P.O. Box 2838
101 Prospect St.
Bellingham, WA 98227
(800) 728-8762

American Gas Index Fund
4922 Fairmont Ave.
Bethesda, MD 20814
(800) 343-3355

American Heritage Fund
31 W. 52nd St., 5th Floor
New York, NY 10019
(212) 474-7308

American Pension Investors
  Trust
P.O. Box 2529
2303 Yorktown Ave.
Lynchburg, VA 24501
(800) 868-6060

Ameritrust's Balanced
  Portfolio
900 Euclid Ave.
Cleveland, OH 44114
(800) 634-4029

Ameritrust's Government
  Securities Portfolio
900 Euclid Ave.
Cleveland, OH 44114
(800) 634-4029

Amev Money Fund Inc.
P.O. Box 64284
St. Paul, MN 55164
(800) 800-AMEV

AMEX Funds
31 W. 52nd St.
New York, NY 10019
(212) 528-2744

Analytic Optioned Equity
  Fund
2222 Martin St., Ste. 230
Irvine, CA 92715
(714) 833-0294

Armstrong Associates Inc.
1445 Ross Ave., LB212
Dallas, TX 75202
(214) 720-9101

Babson Funds
Three Crown Center
2440 Pershing Rd.
Kansas City, MO 64108
(800) 422-2766

Bailard, Biehl & Kaiser Fund
2755 Campus Dr.
San Mateo, CA 94403
(800) 882-8383

The Baker Fund
1601 NW Expy., 20th Floor
Oklahoma City, OK 73118
(800) 937-2257

201

Baron Asset Fund
450 Park Ave., Ste. 2802
New York, NY 10022
(800) 992-2766

Bartlett Funds
36 E. Fourth St.
Cincinnati, OH 45202
(800) 800-4612

Bascom Hill Investors Inc.
6411 Mineral Point Rd.
Madison, WI 53705
(800) 767-0300

Beacon Hill Mutual
    Fund Inc.
75 Federal St., Ste. 403
Boston, MA 02110
(617) 482-0795

Benham Funds
1665 Charleston Rd.
Mountain View, CA 94043
(800) 321-8321

The Berger One Hundred
    Fund
899 Logan St., Ste. 211
Denver, CO 80203
(800) 333-1001

Sanford C. Bernstein Fund
767 Fifth Ave.
New York, NY 10153
(212) 756-4097

The Berwyn Fund Inc.
1189 Lancaster Ave.
Berwyn, PA 19312
(215) 640-4330

Blanchard Funds
41 Madison Ave., 24th Floor
New York, NY 10010
(800) 922-7771

Bond Portfolio for
    Endowments
Four Embarcadero Center,
    Ste. 1800
P.O. Box 7650
San Francisco, CA 94120
(415) 421-9360

The Boston Company Funds
One Boston Place
Boston, MA 02108
(800) 343-6324

Brandywine Blue Fund Inc.
3908 Kennett Pike
P.O. Box 4166
Greenville, DE 19807
(302) 656-3017

Bridges Investment Fund Inc.
8401 W. Dodge Rd.
Omaha, NE 68114
(402) 397-4700

Bruce Fund
20 N. Wacker Dr., Ste. 1425
Chicago, IL 60606
(312) 236-9160

Bull & Bear Funds
11 Hanover Square
New York, NY 10005
(800) 847-4200

Calamos Convertible Income
    Fund
2001 Spring Rd., Ste. 750
Oak Brook, IL 60521
(800) 323-9943

Caldwell Fund Inc.
250 Tampa Ave. W.
P.O. Box 622
Venice, FL 34285
(800) 749-2000

California Investment Trust
    Fund Group
44 Montgomery St.,
    Ste. 2200
San Francisco, CA 94104
(800) 225-8778

California Municipal
    Fund Inc.
111 Broadway, Ste. 1107
New York, NY 10006
(800) 225-6864

Calvert Social Investment
    Fund
1700 Pennsylvania Ave. NW
Washington, DC 20006
(800) 368-2748

Capital Preservation Fund
1665 Charleston Rd.
Mountain View, CA 94043
(800) 321-8321

Cash Equivalent Fund
120 S. LaSalle St.
Chicago, IL 60603
(800) 621-1048

Century Shares Trust
One Liberty Square
Boston, MA 02109
(800) 321-1928

CGM Capital Development
    Fund
P.O. Box 449
Back Bay Annex
Boston, MA 02117
(800) 345-4048

Charter Capital Blue Chip
    Fund
4920 W. Vliet St.
Milwaukee, WI 53208
(414) 257-1842

Citibank IRA Portfolios
153 E. 53rd St.
New York, NY 10043
(800) 248-4472

Clipper Fund Inc.
9601 Wilshire Blvd., Ste. 828
Beverly Hills, CA 90210
(800) 776-5033

CMA Funds
P.O. Box 9011
Princeton, NJ 08543
(800) 262-4636

Columbia Funds
1301 SW 5th Ave.
P.O. Box 1350
Portland, OR 97207
(800) 547-1707

Concord Fund Inc.
55 Temple Pl., 3rd Floor
Boston, MA 02111
(617) 426-3647

Concorde Value Fund
1500 Three Lincoln Centre
5430 LBJ Freeway
Dallas, TX 75240
(800) 338-1579

Connecticut Daily Tax Free
   Income Fund
100 Park Ave., 28th Floor
New York, NY 10017
(800) 221-3079

Copley Fund Inc.
P.O. Box 3287
Fall River, MA 02722
(508) 674-8459

Counsellors Funds
466 Lexington Ave.
New York, NY 10017
(800) 888-6878

Cumberland Growth
   Fund Inc.
26 Broadway, Ste. 205
New York, NY 10004
(800) 543-2620

Daily Funds
100 Park Ave., 20th Floor
New York, NY 10017
(800) 221-3079

Dean Witter/Sears Funds
One World Trade Center
New York, NY 10048
(800) 869-3863

Declaration Cash Account
Ste. 102, Buttonwood Park
435 Devon Park Dr.
Wayne, PA 19087
(800) 423-2345

Delaware Treasury Reserves
1818 Market St.
Philadelphia, PA 19103
(800) 523-4640

The Dividend/Growth
   Fund Inc.
107 N. Adams St.
Rockville, MD 20850
(800) 638-2042

Dodge & Cox Funds
1 Sansome St., 35th Floor
San Francisco, CA 94104
(800) 338-1579

Domini Social Index Trust
6 St. James Ave.
Boston, MA 02116
(800) 762-6814

DR Funds
535 Madison Ave.
New York, NY 10022
(800) 356-6454

Dreman Funds
10 Exchange Pl., Ste. 2050
Jersey City, NJ 07302
(800) 533-1608

Dreyfus Funds
EAB Plaza
144 Glenn Curtis Blvd.,
   Plaza Level
Uniondale, NY 11556
(800) 645-6561

Dupree Funds
P.O. Box 1149
Lexington, KY 40589
(800) 866-0614

Eclipse Balanced Fund
144 E. 30th St.
New York, NY 10016
(800) 872-2710

Elfun Funds
3003 Summer St.
P.O. Box 120074
Stamford, CT 06912
(800) 242-0134

Endowments Inc.
Four Embarcadero Center,
   Ste. 1800
P.O. Box 7650
San Francisco, CA 94120
(415) 421-9360

Equity Strategies Fund Inc.
767 Third Ave., 5th Floor
New York, NY 10017
(212) 888-6685

The Evergreen Funds
2500 Westchester Ave.
Purchase, NY 10577
(800) 235-0064

Fairmont Fund
1346 S. Third St.
Louisville, KY 40208
(800) 262-9936

Fasciano Fund Inc.
190 S. LaSalle St.,
   Ste. 2800
Chicago, IL 60603
(800) 338-1579

Federated Funds
Federated Investors Tower
Pittsburgh, PA 15222
(800) 245-5000

FFB Equity Fund Inc.
230 Park Ave.
New York, NY 10169
(800) 845-8406

Fidelity Funds
82 Devonshire St.
Boston, MA 02109
(800) 544-8888

Fiduciary Funds
222 E. Mason St.
Milwaukee, WI 53202
(800) 338-1579

Financial Funds
7800 E. Union Ave., Ste. 800
Denver, CO 80237
(800) 525-8085

First Eagle Fund of
    America Inc.
45 Broadway
New York, NY 10006
(800) 451-3623

First Government Money
    Market
4550 Montgomery Ave.
Bethesda, MD 20814
(800) 368-2748

Flagship Basic Value Fund
One First National Plaza,
    Ste. 910
Dayton, OH 45402
(800) 227-4648

The Flex-Funds
6000 Memorial Dr.
P.O. Box 7177
Dublin, OH 43017
(800) 325-3539

Fontaine Capital
    Appreciation Fund
111 S. Calvert St., Ste. 1550
Baltimore, MD 21202
(800) 247-1550

The 44 Wall St. Equity
    Fund Inc.
26 Broadway, Ste. 205
New York, NY 10004
(800) 543-2620

Founders Funds
3033 E. First Ave., Ste. 810
Denver, CO 80206
(800) 525-2440

Fund for Tax-Free
    Investors Inc.
4922 Fairmont Ave.
Bethesda, MD 20814
(800) 343-3355

Fundamental Fixed Income
    Municipal Series
90 Washington
New York, NY 10006
(800) 225-6864

Fundtrust Funds
452 Fifth Ave.
New York, NY 10018
(800) 344-9033

Gabelli Funds
655 Third Ave.
New York, NY 10117
(800) 422-3554

Galaxy Funds
One Boston Place
Boston, MA 02108
(800) 441-7379

Gateway Funds
400 TechneCenter Dr. #220
Milford, OH 45150
(800) 354-6339

GE S&S Long Term
   Interest Fund
3003 Summer St.
P.O. Box 7900
Stamford, CT 06904
(203) 326-2300

General Funds (Dreyfus)
EAB Plaza
144 Glenn Curtis Blvd.,
   Plaza Level
Uniondale, NY 11556
(800) 242-8671

Gintel Funds
Greenwich Office Park, #6
Greenwich, CT 06830
(800) 243-5808

GIT Trusts
1655 N. Fort Myer Dr.,
   Ste. 1000
Arlington, VA 22209
(800) 336-3063

Gradison Trusts
The 580 Building
580 Walnut St.
Cincinnati, OH 45202
(800) 869-5999

Greenfield Fund Inc.
230 Park Ave., Ste. 910
New York, NY 10169
(212)986-2600

Greenspring Fund Inc.
Ste. 322, The Quadrangle
Village of Cross Keys
Baltimore, MD 21131
(301) 435-9000

Growth Industry Shares Inc.
135 S. LaSalle St.
Chicago, IL 60603
(800) 621-0687

Harbor Funds
One SeaGate
Toledo, OH 43666
(800) 422-1050

Hawaii Pacific Fund Inc.
188 Bishop St., Ste. 1201
Honolulu, HI 96813
(808) 521-4831

Helmsman Funds
1900 E. Dublin-Granville Rd.
Columbus, OH 43229
(800) 338-4345

The Highmark Group
1900 E. Dublin-Granville Rd.
Columbus, OH 43229
(800) 433-6884

IAI Funds
1100 Dain Tower
P.O. Box 357
Minneapolis, MN 55440
(800) 927-3863

Ivy Funds
40 Industrial Park Rd.
Hingham, MA 02043
(800) 235-3322

Janus Funds
100 Fillmore St., Ste. 300
Denver, CO 80206
(800) 525-3713

Japan Fund Inc.
160 Federal St.
Boston, MA 02110
(800) 535-2726

Kaufmann Fund
17 Battery Pl., Ste. 2624
New York, NY 10004
(212) 344-2661

Kemper Money Market
  Fund Inc.
120 S. LaSalle St.
Chicago, IL 60603
(800) 621-1048

Kidder Peabody Money
  Funds
20 Exchange Place
New York, NY 10005
(212) 510-5351

Kleinwort Benson
  International Equity Fund
200 Park Ave., 24th Floor
New York, NY 10166
(800) 237-4218

Landmark Funds
6 St. James Ave., 9th Floor
Boston, MA 02116
(800) 223-4447

Lazard Special Equity
  Fund Inc.
1 Rockefeller Plaza,
  Ste. 2400
New York, NY 10020
(800) 854-8525

Legg Mason Funds
111 S. Calvert St.
P.O. Box 1476
Baltimore, MD 21203
(800) 822-5544

Lepercoq-Istel Trust
345 Park Ave.
New York, NY 10154
(800) 548-7878

Lexington Funds
P.O. Box 1515
Park 80 W., Plaza Two
Saddle Brook, NJ 07662
(800) 526-0056

Liberty U.S. Government
   Money Market Trust
Federated Investors Tower
Pittsburgh, PA 15222
(800) 245-5000

Lindner Dividend Fund Inc.
7711 Carondelet, Ste. 700
P.O. Box 11208
St. Louis, MO 63105
(314) 727-5305

Liquid Capital Income Trust
1228 Euclid Ave., Ste. 1100
Cleveland, OH 44115
(800) 321-2322

LMH Fund, Ltd.
544 Riverside Ave.
Westport, CT 06880
(800) 422-2564

Mairs & Power Growth
   Fund Inc.
W-2062 First National
   Bank Bldg.
St. Paul, MN 55101
(612) 222-8478

Mariner Funds
250 Park Ave.
New York, NY 10177
(800) 634-2536

MAS Pooled Trust Fund
   Portfolios
c/o The Vanguard Group Inc.
P.O. Box 1102
Valley Forge, PA 19482
(800) 332-5577

Mathers Fund Inc.
100 Corporate N., Ste. 201
Bannockburn, IL 60015
(800) 962-3863

Maxus Equity Fund
3350 Lander Rd.
Cleveland, OH 44124
(216) 292-3434

The Merger Fund
11 High Meadows
Mt. Kisco, NY 10549
(914) 241-3360

Meridian Fund Inc.
60 E. Sir Francis Drake
   Blvd., Ste. 306
Larkspur, CA 94939
(800) 446-6662

Merrill Lynch Ready
   Assets Trust
P.O. Box 9011
Princeton, NJ 08543
(800) 221-7210

Merriman Funds
1200 Westlake Ave. N.,
    Ste. 700
Seattle, WA 98109
(800) 423-4893

MetLife — State Street
    Government Income Fund
One Financial Center,
    30th Floor
Boston, MA 02111
(800) 882-0052

Michigan Daily Income
    Fund Inc.
100 Park Ave., 28th Floor
New York, NY 10017
(800) 221-3079

Mim Funds
4500 Rockside Rd., #440
Independence, OH 44131
(800) 233-1240

Monetta Fund Inc.
1776-B S. Naperville Rd.,
    Ste. 207
Wheaton, IL 60187
(800) 666-3882

Money Market Management
    Inc.
Federated Investors Tower
Pittsburgh, PA 15222
(800) 245-5000

Mutual Series Funds
51 John F. Kennedy Pkwy.
Short Hills, NJ 07078
(800) 448-3863

National Industries Fund Inc.
5990 Greenwood Plaza Blvd.
Englewood, CO 80111
(800) 367-7814

National Liquid Reserves
    Funds
1345 Avenue of the Americas
New York, NY 10105
(800) 223-7078

Neuberger & Berman Funds
342 Madison Ave.
New York, NY 10173
(800) 877-9700

Neuwirth Fund Inc.
140 Broadway, 42nd Floor
New York, NY 10005
(800) 225-8011

New England Funds
399 Boylston St.
Boston, MA 02116
(800) 343-7104

New York Daily Income
    Fund
100 Park Ave., 28th Floor
New York, NY 10017
(800) 221-3079

New York Life Funds Inc.
51 Madison Ave.
New York, NY 10010
(800) 695-2126

New York Municipal
   Fund Inc.
90 Washington
New York, NY 10006
(800) 225-6864

Newton Funds
330 E. Kilbourn Ave.
2 Plaza E., Ste. 1150
Milwaukee, WI 53202
(800) 247-7039

Nicholas Funds
700 N. Water St., Ste. 1010
Milwaukee, WI 53202
(800) 227-5987

Nomura Pacific Basin
   Fund Inc.
180 Maden Ln.
New York, NY 10038
(800) 833-0018

Northeast Investors Growth
   Fund
50 Congress St., Ste. 1000
Boston, MA 02109
(800) 225-6704

Permanent Portfolio Funds
207 Jefferson Square
P.O. Box 5847
Austin, TX 78763
(800) 531-5142

Perritt Capital Growth
   Fund Inc.
680 N. Lake Shore Dr.,
   Ste. 2038
Chicago, IL 60611
(800) 338-1579

Pierpont Capital Appreciation
   Fund
1221 Avenue of the Americas
New York, NY 10020
(800) 521-5412

Pimco Trust Portfolios
840 Newport Center, Ste. 360
P.O. Box 9000
Newport Beach, CA 92660
(800) 443-6915

Pine Street Fund Inc.
140 Broadway, 42nd Floor
New York, NY 10005
(800) 225-8011

Pinnacle Fund
36 S. Pennsylvania St.,
   Ste. 610
Indianapolis, IN 46204
(317) 633-4080

Portico Funds
207 E. Buffalo St., Ste. 315
Milwaukee, WI 53202
(800) 228-1024

T. Rowe Price Funds
100 E. Pratt St.
Baltimore, MD 21202
(800) 225-5132

Primary Trend Funds
First Financial Center
700 N. Water St.
Milwaukee, WI 53202
(800) 443-6544

Primecap Fund
P.O. Box 2600
Valley Forge, PA 19482
(800) 662-2739

The Prudent Speculator Fund
P.O. Box 75231
Los Angeles, CA 90075
(800) 444-4778

Prudential-Bache Securities
One Seaport Plaza
New York, NY 10292
(800) 225-1852

The Rainbow Fund Inc.
19 Rector St.
New York, NY 10006
(212) 509-8532

Reich & Tang Equity Fund
100 Park Ave.
New York, NY 10017
(800) 221-3079

Reserve Funds
810 Seventh Ave.
New York, NY 10019
(800) 223-5547

Reynolds Blue Chip
   Growth Fund
Wood Island, 3rd Floor
80 E. Sir Francis Drake
   Blvd., Ste. 3A
Larkspur, CA 94939
(800) 338-1579

The Rightime Fund
The First Pavilion, Ste. 1000
Wyncote, PA 19095
(800) 242-1421

RMA Funds
1285 Avenue of the Americas
New York, NY 10019
(800) 762-1000

Robertson Stephens
   Growth Fund
One Embarcadero Center,
   Ste. 3100
San Francisco, CA 94111
(800) 766-3863

The Rockwood Growth Fund
545 Shoup Ave., #243
P.O. Box 50313
Idaho Falls, ID 83405
(208) 522-5593

Rushmore Funds
4922 Fairmont Ave.
Bethesda, MD 20814
(800) 343-3355

Safeco Funds
P.O. Box 34890
Seattle, WA 34890
(800) 624-5711

Salomon Brothers
  Opportunity Fund Inc.
7 World Trade Center,
  38th Floor
New York, NY 10048
(800) 225-6666

SBSF Funds
45 Rockefeller Plaza
New York, NY 10111
(800) 422-7273

Schroder Capital Funds
787 Seventh Ave.
New York, NY 10019
(800) 344-8332

Schwab Funds
101 Montgomery St.
San Francisco, CA 94104
(800) 526-8600

Scudder Funds
160 Federal St.
Boston, MA 02110
(800) 225-2470

Seafirst Retirement Portfolio
P.O. Box 84248
Seattle, WA 98124
(800) 323-9919

SEI Funds
680 E. Swedesford Rd.
Wayne, PA 19087
(800) 342-5734

Selected Funds
1228 Euclid Ave.
Cleveland, OH 44115
(800) 367-2098

Sequoia Fund Inc.
1370 Avenue of the Americas
New York, NY 10019
(212) 245-4500

SFT Odd Lot Fund
1016 W. 8th Ave., Ste. D
King of Prussia, PA 19406
(800) 523-2044

Shadow Stock Fund
Three Crown Center
2440 Pershing Rd.
Kansas City, MO 64108
(800) 422-2766

Sherman, Dean Fund Inc.
6061 NW Expy., Ste. 465
San Antonio, TX 78201
(800) 247-6375

Short Term Income Fund
100 Park Ave.
New York, NY 10017
(800) 221-3079

SIT "New Beginning" Funds
4600 Norwest Center
90 S. 7th St.
Minneapolis, MN 55402
(800) 332-5580

Smith Hayes Trust Inc.
500 Centre Terrace
1225 L St.
Lincoln, NE 68508
(800) 279-7437

Sound Shore Fund Inc.
8 Sound Shore Dr.
Greenwich, CT 06836
(800) 221-3079

Southeastern Asset
  Management Fund
860 Ridgelake Blvd.,
  Ste. 301
Memphis, TN 38120
(800) 445-9469

Special Portfolios Inc.
P.O. Box 64284
St. Paul, MN 55164
(800) 800-AMEV

State Farm Funds
One State Farm Plaza
Bloomington, IL 61710
(309) 766-2029

Steadman Funds
1730 K St., NW,
  Ste. 904
Washington, DC 20006
(800) 424-8570

Steinroe Funds
300 W. Adams
Chicago, IL 60606
(800) 338-2550

Stralem Fund
405 Park Ave.
New York, NY 10022
(212) 888-8123

Stratton Growth Fund
Plymouth Meeting Executive
  Campus
610 W. Germantown Pike,
  Ste. 361
Plymouth Meeting, PA
  19462
(800) 634-5726

Strong Funds
100 Heritage Reserve
P.O. Box 2936
Milwaukee, WI 53201
(800) 368-3863

Sunshine Growth Trust
1842 Sabre St.
Hayward, CA 94545
(415) 782-3297

Tax-Free Instruments Trust
Federated Investors Tower
Pittsburgh, PA 15222-3779
(800) 245-5000

The Tax-Free Money Fund
1345 Avenue of the Americas
New York, NY 10105
(800) 221-8806

Thompson, Unger & Plumb
8201 Excelsior Dr.
Madison, WI 53717
(800) 338-1579

Treasury First Inc.
1661 Lincoln Blvd., Ste. 400
Santa Monica, CA 90404
(213) 392-4331

Trustees' Commingled Fund
P.O. Box 2600
Valley Forge, PA 19482
(800) 662-2739

Twentieth Century Funds
4500 Main St.
P.O. Box 419200
Kansas City, MO 64141
(800) 345-2021

UMB Funds
Three Crown Center
2440 Pershing Rd.
Kansas City, MO 64108
(800) 422-2766

United Services Funds
P.O. Box 29467
San Antonio, TX 78229
(800) 873-8637

U.S. Boston Foreign Growth
 and Income Series
Lincoln North
Lincoln, MA 01773
(800) 331-1244

USAA Funds
USAA Bldg.
San Antonio, TX 78288
(800) 531-8181

UST Master Funds
One Boston Place
Boston, MA 02108
(800) 446-1012

Valley Forge Fund Inc.
1375 Anthony Wayne Dr.
Wayne, PA 19087
(800) 548-1942

Value Line Funds
711 Third Ave.
New York, NY 10017
(800) 223-0818

Vanguard Funds
P.O. Box 2600
Valley Forge, PA 19482
(800) 662-2739

Vantage Money Market
    Funds
1345 Avenue of the Americas
New York, NY 10105
(800) 221-3434

Variable Stock Fund
1414 Main St., 12th Floor
Springfield, MA 01144
(800) 343-2902

Volumetric Fund Inc.
87 Violet Dr.
Pearl River, NY 10965
(800) 541-3863

Wade Fund Inc.
5100 Poplar Ave., Ste. 2224
Memphis, TN 38137
(901) 682-4613

Wasatch Funds
68 S. Main St., Ste. 400
Salt Lake City, UT 84101
(800) 345-7460

Wayne Hummer Growth
    Fund Trust
175 W. Jackson Blvd.
Chicago, IL 60604
(800) 621-4477

Webster Cash Reserve Fund
20 Exchange Place
New York, NY 10005
(212) 510-5041

Weitz Series Fund Inc.
9290 W. Dodge Rd., #405
Omaha, NE 68114
(402) 391-1980

Wellesley Income Fund
P.O. Box 2600
Valley Forge, PA 19482
(800) 662-2739

Wellington Fund
P.O. Box 2600
Valley Forge, PA 19482
(800) 662-2739

Wells Fargo Investment Trust
525 Market St., Ste. 1900
San Francisco, CA 94105
(800) 835-5472

Weston Portfolios
45 William St.
Wellesley Office Park,
    Ste. 100
Wellesley, MA 02181
(617) 239-0445

The Wexford Trust
12300 Perry Hwy.
P.O. Box 598
Wexford, PA 15090
(412) 935-5520

Windsor Fund
P.O. Box 2600
Valley Forge, PA 19482
(800) 662-2739

Working Assets Money Fund
230 California St., Ste. 500
San Francisco, CA 94111
(800) 533-FUND

Child Support Enforcement Agencies

Alabama
Child Support Enforcement
   Division
Department of Human
   Resources
64 N. Union St.
Montgomery, AL 36130
(205) 242-2734

Alaska
Child Support Enforcement
   Division
Department of Revenue
660 W. 7th Ave., 4th Floor
Anchorage, AK 99501
(907) 276-3441

Arizona
Child Support Enforcement
   Administration
Department of Economic
   Security
222 W. Encanto
P.O. Box 5123 — Site
   Code 776A
Phoenix, AZ 85005
(602) 275-0236

Arkansas
Division of Child Support
   Enforcement
Arkansas Social Services
P.O. Box 3358
Little Rock, AR 72203
(501) 682-8398

California
Child Support Program
   Management Branch
Department of Social
   Services
744 P St.
Mail Stop 9-011
Sacramento, CA 95814
(916) 322-8495

Colorado
Division of Child Support
   Enforcement
Department of Social
   Services
1575 Sherman St.
Denver, CO 80203-1714
(303) 866-5994

Connecticut
Bureau of Child Support
 Enforcement
Department of Human
 Resources
1049 Asylum Ave.
Hartford, CT 06105
(203) 566-3053

Delaware
Division of Child Support
 Enforcement
Department of Health and
 Social Services
P.O. Box 904
New Castle, DE 10720
(302) 421-8300

District of Columbia
Office of Paternity and Child
 Support
Department of Human
 Services
3rd Floor, Ste. 3013
425 I St., NW
Washington, D.C. 20001
(202) 724-5610

Florida
Office of Child Support
 Enforcement
Department of Health and
 Rehabilitative Services
1317 Winewood Blvd.,
 Bldg. 3
Tallahassee, FL 32399-0700
(904) 488-9900

Georgia
Office of Child Support
 Recovery
State Department of Human
 Resources
878 Peachtree St., NE
Room 529
Atlanta, GA 30309
(404) 894-4119

Guam
Office of the Attorney
 General
Child Support Enforcement
 Office
Union Bank Bldg.,
 Ste. 309
194 Hernan Cortez Ave.
Agana, Guam 96910
(671) 477-2036

Hawaii
Child Support Enforcement
 Agency
Department of the
 Attorney General
P.O. Box 1860
Honolulu, HI 96805-1860
(808) 548-5779

Idaho
Bureau of Child Support
    Enforcement
Department of Health and
    Welfare
450 W. State St.
Towers Bldg., 7th Floor
Boise, ID 83720
(208) 334-5710

Illinois
Division of Child Support
    Enforcement
Department of Public Aid
Prescott E. Bloom Bldg.
201 S. Grand Ave. E.
P.O. Box 19405
Springfield, IL 62794-9405
(217) 782-1366

Indiana
Child Support Enforcement
    Division
Department of Public
    Welfare
4th Floor
141 S. Meridian St.
Indianapolis, IN 46225
(317) 232-4885

Iowa
Bureau of Collections
Iowa Department of Human
    Services
Hoover Bldg., 5th Floor
Des Moines, IA 50319
(515) 281-5580

Kansas
Child Support Enforcement
    Program
Department of Social and
    Rehabilitation Services
Biddle Bldg.
300 SW Oakley St.
P.O. Box 497
Topeka, KS 66603
(913) 296-3237

Kentucky
Division of Child Support
    Enforcement
Department of Social
    Insurance
Cabinet for Human
    Resources
275 E. Main St.
6th Floor E.
Frankfort, KY 40621
(502) 564-2285

Louisiana
Support Enforcement
    Services
Department of Social
    Services
P.O. Box 94065
Baton Rouge, LA 70804
(504) 342-4780

Maine
Support Enforcement and
  Location Unit
Bureau of Social Welfare
Department of Human
  Services
State House, Station 11
Augusta, ME 04333
(207) 289-2886

Maryland
Child Support Enforcement
  Administration
Department of Human
  Resources
311 W. Saratoga St.
Baltimore, MD 21201
(301) 333-3979

Massachusetts
Child Support Enforcement
  Division
Department of Revenue
215 1st St.
Cambridge, MA 02124
(617) 621-4200

Michigan
Office of Child Support
Department of Social
  Services
300 S. Capitol Ave.
Ste. 621
P.O. Box 30037
Lansing, MI 48909
(517) 373-7570

Minnesota
Office of Child Support
  Enforcement
Department of Human
  Services
444 Lafayette Rd.
4th Floor
St. Paul, MN 55155-3846
(612) 296-2499

Mississippi
Child Support Division
State Department of Public
  Welfare
515 E. Amite St.
P.O. Box 352
Jackson, MS 39205
(601) 354-0341, ext. 503

Missouri
Department of Social
  Services
Division of Child Support
  Enforcement
P.O. Box 1527
Jefferson City, MO
  65102-1527
(406) 444-4614

Montana
Child Support Enforcement
  Division
Department of Social and
  Rehabilitation Services
P.O. Box 5955
Helena, MT 59604
(406) 444-4614

Nebraska
Child Support Enforcement
  Office
Department of Social
  Services
P.O. Box 950226
Lincoln, NE 68509
(402) 471-9125

Nevada
Child Support Enforcement
  Program
Department of Human
  Resources
2527 N. Carson St.
Capital Complex
Carson City, NV 89710
(702) 885-4744

New Hampshire
Office of Child Support
  Enforcement Services
Division of Welfare
Health and Welfare Bldg.
6 Hazen Dr.
Concord, NH 03301
(603) 271-4426

New Jersey
Division of Economic
  Assistance
Department of Human
  Services
Bureau of Child Support and
  Paternity Programs
CN 716
Trenton, NJ 08625
(609) 588-2401

New Mexico
Child Support Enforcement
  Division
Department of Human
  Services
P.O. Box 25109
Santa Fe, NM 87504
(505) 827-7200

New York
Office of Child Support
  Enforcement
New York State Department
  of Social Services
P.O. Box 14
One Commerce Plaza
Albany, NY 12260
(518) 474-9081

North Carolina
Child Support Enforcement
  Section
Division of Social Services
Department of Human
  Resources
437 N. Harrington St.
Raleigh, NC 27603-1393
(919) 733-4120

North Dakota
Child Support Enforcement
  Agency
Department of Human
  Services
State Capitol
Bismarck, ND 58505
(701) 224-3582

Ohio
Bureau of Child Support
Department of Human
 Services
State Office Tower,
 27th Floor
30 E. Broad St.
Columbus, OH 43266-0423
(614) 466-3233

Oklahoma
Child Support Enforcement
 Division
Department of Human
 Services
P.O. Box 25352
Oklahoma City, OK 73125
(405) 424-5871

Oregon
Recovery Services Section
Adult and Family Services
 Division
Department of Human
 Resources
P.O. Box 14506
Salem, OR 97309
(503) 378-5439

Pennsylvania
Bureau of Child Support
 Enforcement
Department of Public
 Welfare
P.O. Box 8018
Harrisburg, PA 17105
(717) 787-3672
 or (717) 783-5184

Puerto Rico
Child Support Enforcement
 Program
Department of Social
 Services
Call Box 3349
San Juan, PR 00904
(809) 722-4731

Rhode Island
Bureau of Family Support
Department of Human
 Services
77 Dorrance St.
Providence, RI 02903
(401) 277-2409

South Carolina
Child Support Enforcement
 Division
Department of Social
 Services
P.O. Box 1520
Columbia, SC 29202-9988
(803) 737-5870

South Dakota
Office of Child Support
 Enforcement
Department of Social
 Services
700 Governors Dr.
Pierre, SD 57501-2291
(605) 773-3641

Tennessee
Child Support Services
Department of Human
 Services
Citizens Plaza Bldg.
12th Floor
400 Deadrick St.
Nashville, TN 37219
(615) 741-1820

Texas
Child Support Enforcement
 Division
Office of the Attorney
 General
P.O. Box 12548
Austin, TX 78711-2548
(512) 463-2181

Utah
Office of Recovery Services
Department of Social
 Services
P.O. Box 45011
Salt Lake City, UT 84145
(801) 538-4400

Vermont
Child Support Division
Department of Social
 Welfare
103 S. Main St.
Waterbury, VT 05676
(802) 241-2910

Virgin Islands
Support and Paternity
 Division
Department of Law
46 Norre Gade St.
St. Thomas, VI 00801
(809) 776-0372

Virginia
Division of Support
 Enforcement Program
Department of Social
 Services
8007 Discovery Dr.
Richmond, VA 23288
(804) 662-9297

Washington
Revenue Division
Department of Social and
 Health Services
Mail Stop HJ-31
Olympia, WA 98504
(206) 586-6111

West Virginia
Child Advocate Office
Department of Human
 Services
1900 Washington St., E.
Charleston, WV 25305
(304) 348-3780

Wisconsin
Division of Economic
   Support
Bureau of Child Support
1 W. Wilson St., Room 382
P.O. Box 7935
Madison, WI 53707-7935
(608) 266-1175

Wyoming
Child Support Enforcement
   Section
Division of Public Assistance
   and Social Services
State Department of Health
   and Social Services
Hathaway Blvd.
Cheyenne, WY 82002
(307) 777-7892

Author's note: Some of these terms do not appear in this book. However, as you familiarize yourself with financial matters and read financial publications, you will run across all of this terminology.

Adjustable rate mortgage. A mortgage agreement between a financial institution and an individual that allows for adjustments to the interest rates at specified intervals. These adjustments are usually tied to an index such as the interest rate on U.S. Treasury bills or average mortgage rates nationally. The agreement usually provides for a cap or limit to the rate increase, both annually and for the life of the loan.

These loans are usually a good strategy when interest rates are high because a lower initial rate can be acquired and later the loan can be converted or refinanced when overall rates are lower. It is commonly referred to as ARM.

Agent. A representative; one who is authorized to act on behalf of another.

Amortization. Payment of a debt by regular installment payments.

Annuity. These investment vehicles are usually divided into two categories: fixed and variable. Fixed annuities provide a guaranteed rate of return for a fixed period of time, usually one, three or five years. Variable annuities provide the opportunity for the investor to choose from various portfolios. These portfolios are similar to mutual funds. Variable annuities usually are better for individuals investing for a long period of time. This is because they allow for participation in the stock, bond or international markets which have historically outpaced inflation.

Assumption of mortgage. The taking over of an existing mortgage by a buyer.

Balanced mutual fund. A mutual fund that buys stocks, bonds and money markets. These portfolios are known for providing for a higher degree of safety in exchange for lower overall returns. Individuals looking for higher returns are usually attracted to specific mutual funds (for example, stock funds, bond funds, international funds). These funds permit more concentrated results and require more active involvement because they are more sensitive to market fluctuations. Balanced mutual funds are a good alternative for individuals seeking a low level of involvement as well as stability in a variety of market conditions.

Balloon mortgage. A form of financing which requires periodic payments and a final large (balloon) payment to satisfy the loan.

Bankruptcy. A state of insolvency of an individual or corporation. U.S. bankruptcy laws provide for the inability to repay debts. There are two primary forms of personal bankruptcy: Chapter 7 and Chapter 13. A business may file for a Chapter 11 bankruptcy. The basic difference between these is that Chapter 7 does not provide for the repayment of creditors and usually involves the discharging of debt. Chapter 11 and Chapter 13 require a reorganization of debt, which involves creating a plan to repay the debt. Some items that are typically negotiated are interest rate, payment period and other terms of the loan agreement.

Bond. Also known as debenture, a bond is issued by a corporation or government. These debt instruments provide for a specific date of repayment, known as the maturity date, and for periodic interest payments.

Corporate and municipal bonds are rated by Moody's, a bond rating service. A Moody rating is an evaluation of the ability of the issuer to repay the debt. U.S. Treasury securities are not rated because they are backed by the U.S. government. The highest rating that can be received from Moody's is AAA.

Municipal bonds are free from state income tax if the recipient of the interest payments is a resident of the municipality's state. U.S. Treasury securities are exempt from state and local income tax.

Buyer's market. The supply of available properties exceeds the demand.

Capital gain. The positive difference between an asset's purchase price and its selling price. In the event that the sales price is lower than the purchase price, it is referred to as a capital loss. As of 1986 capital gains are taxed at the same rate as regular income.

Certificate of deposit. A debt instrument issued by a bank. In most cases CDs are available in a wide range of maturities and are protected through government insurance. The rates paid to the depositor vary based on economic conditions and competitiveness in the marketplace.

Collateral. An asset pledged as security to a lender until a debt is repaid. This is most common in the area of home mortgages and automobiles. Loans that do not require collateral are called unsecured loans, common examples of which are credit cards and personal lines of credit.

Collectibles. Items purchased by specialized collectors. These items include coins, stamps, baseball cards, albums, photographs and antiques. Although the buyers of these items perceive them as investments, they typically make poor investments because of the markup from the dealer to the consumer. Additionally, risk is present because fads, which create increases in the price of these objects, are unpredictable. Most experts in the investment community would not recommend this area unless an individual has a high level of expertise.

Commodities contract. These speculative investments are often referred to as futures or options on futures. This investment area allows the investor to speculate on the future price of items such as grain, metal, oil and various foods, such as citrus and coffee. Most individuals who invest in commodities are trying to hedge other existing investments. For example, a citrus farmer could buy citrus futures so that if a severe freeze wipes out his crop, his contract would pay him a compensating profit. Because of the high degree of risk involved in these investments, they are not recommended for the novice.

Consumer Protection Act of 1968. Federal legislation that requires fair and proper disclosure from lender to consumer. Such details as annual percentage rate, special loan terms and so on must be openly disclosed.

Credit rating. An established record of the payment history of an individual or corporation. These records are retained by credit bureaus, which provide this information to their members to assist them in making an evaluation on the credit risk of a loan.

Equity. The difference between the amount of indebtedness and the market value of an asset. The term *equity* is typically referred to in relation to a home.

Estate tax. Tax imposed on assets left to heirs in a will. Current tax laws allow for an exclusion from federal estate taxes on the first $600,000 of assets. Through the use of a trust, this amount can be increased to $1.2 million.

Fair market value. The price at which an asset can be readily sold.

General lien. A claim that may affect all of the properties of a debtor.

Ginnie Mae. Nickname for Government National Mortgage Association. These mortgage-backed securities provide funds for banks to lend for home purchases. These are sometimes referred to as pass-through securities, which refers to the fact that a bank will make a loan and then sell it on the secondary market. One note of caution: Ginnie

Maes give monthly payments of both principal and interest to the investor. This means that part of your monthly payment is the return of your original investment.

High-yield bonds. Known as junk bonds, these debt instruments are typically high-yielding and low-rated, meaning they carry more risk of default than a bond with a higher rating. Bonds rated BB or lower are referred to as junk. Although these bonds are high risk, they are sometimes recommended in mutual funds where the diversification allows for a partial diffusing of this risk.

Inflation. Rise of cost in consumer goods and services.

IRA. See "Self-directed IRA."

Joint tenancy. An estate or interest owned by more than one person, each having equal rights to possession and enjoyment.

Junk bonds. See "High-yield bonds."

Lease. A contract involving the rental of an asset. This can be real estate, equipment, automobiles, and the like.

Leverage. The use of borrowed funds to finance the purchase of an asset.

Loan to value (LTV) ratio. The ratio of a mortgage loan in relation to the value of the property.

Margin account. An account that allows the investor to borrow funds from the brokerage firm to buy securities. Federal law restricts an individual from borrowing more than 50 percent of the purchase price of a security. Margin accounts are typically used in bull markets, where the cost of borrowing can be easily exceeded because of increasing stock prices. This type of account is recommended only for aggressive, seasoned investors.

Mortgage broker. One who finds a mortgage lender for a borrower.

National Association of Securities Dealers. A nonprofit organization that supervises the sales practices of broker/dealer firms in the United States.

Over-improvement. An addition or improvement to a property that causes the value of that property to exceed a reasonable future sales price that would make the improvement recoverable.

Penny stock. A stock that sells for less than $5 per share. These stocks are usually new issues and are very risky but offer tremendous potential for increasing in value.

Prepayment clause. A provision in a mortgage that allows the mortgagee to reduce the debt at an accelerated pace without penalty.

Second mortgage. A loan that follows a first mortgage, typically on a house. It is normally taken out when the borrower needs more money.

Sector fund. A specialized mutual fund that invests in a specific industry. Groups that have such funds available are Fidelity and Financial Funds. Some of these sectors are energy, retail and biotechnology.

Securities and Exchange Commission. The federal agency set up to regulate the purchase and sale of securities in the United States.

Self-directed IRA. An individual retirement account that allows an individual the privilege to make his or her own investment choices, thereby allowing for maximum flexibility of investment options.

Seller's market. The demand for available properties exceeds the supply.

Tax credit. A dollar-for-dollar tax reduction.

Tax deduction. An amount subtracted from taxable income. It is worth less than a tax credit.

Title insurance. An insurance policy that protects the holder from any hidden claims against property.

Uniform Gift to Minors Act. A federal law that allows for proper management of assets for the benefit of a minor until that minor reaches the age of legal adulthood.

Allen, Robert. *Nothing Down*. New York, N.Y.: Simon and Schuster, 1984.

Cassidy, Daniel. *The Complete Guide to Scholarships*. Englewood Cliffs, N.J.: Prentice Hall, 1992.

Dacey, Norman. *How to Avoid Probate*. New York, N.Y.: Crown Publishers, Inc., 1983.

Dolan, Ken, and Daria Dolan. *Smart Money*. New York, N.Y.: Berkley Publishing Group, 1990.

Eisenson, Marc. *The Banker's Secret*. New York, N.Y.: Villard Books, 1991.

Graves, Warrick, and Joseph Leff. *Stop Probate Now*. Overland Park, Kans.: Trust Publishing Company, 1991.

Hardy, Dorcas, and Joseph Colburn. *Social Insecurity*. New York, N.Y.: Villard Books, 1991.

Lesko, Matthew. *Lesko's Info-Power*. Kensington, Md.: Info USA, 1990.

Loritz, Len. *No Fault Negotiating*. New York, N.Y.: Warner Books, Inc., 1987.

Milton, Arthur. *How Your Life Insurance Policies Rob You*. New York, N.Y.: Citadel Press, 1980.

Parrish, Darrell. *The Car Buyer's Art*. Bell Flower, Calif.: Book Express, 1989.

Pilot, Kevin. *Credit Approved*. Holdbrook, Mass.: Bob Adams, Inc., 1992.

Polto, Pearl. *Pearl Polto's Easy Guide to Good Credit*. New York, N.Y.: Berkley Publishing Group, 1990.

Ross, Charles. *The Best of Your Personal Finance*. Atlanta, Ga.: FMF Publishing Company, 1991.

Savage, Terry. *Terry Savage Talks Money*. New York, N.Y.: HarperCollins Publishers, 1990.

Stewardship Counseling

Contact James L. Paris Financial Services to speak with a stewardship consultant at (800) 950-PLAN. James L. Paris Financial Services is a fee-based financial planning firm based in Central Florida.

(Services not available in all states.)

The Insurance Shopping Network
$24.95

Are you looking for the best rates on term life and health insurance coverage for you and your family? Stop! Look no further.

The typical Christian consumer is sold insurance without ever getting quotes from other qualified carriers. That is why Jim Paris designed the Insurance Shopping Network to do just that — shop from a national network of qualified carriers to provide you, the consumer, with the best coverage available.

The Insurance Shopping Network does not sell insurance — it simply scans our nearly limitless database to search for your coverage needs at the lowest price.

If we cannot find you the best rates on term life and/or health insurance coverage, we will refund your money.

Call (800) 829-4037.

The American Dream
$16.95 + $3 shipping and handling

Jim Paris teams up with attorney J.W. Dicks to help consumers attain their financial goals. Hardcover book addresses ten proven principles for financial freedom.

Boot Camp Three-Night Seminar
$39.95 + $3 shipping and handling

Experience Jim Paris's live TV seminar on three one-hour videos. Jim teaches proper financial stewardship principles found in Matthew 25.

Estate Planning
$19.95 + $3 shipping and handling

In this video Jim Paris explains the value of proper estate planning in easy-to-understand nontechnical language.

Financial Boot Camp for Single Christians
$9.95 + $3 shipping and handling

A one-hour audiotape designed to help single Christians of all ages survive the economically turbulent times.

Financial Boot Camp Software
$49 + $3 shipping and handling

Financial Boot Camp software makes it simple and easy to handle your financial and investment needs properly. With it you can access accounting functions, check writing, budget creation and maintenance, mortgage amortization schedules, a financial calculator and investment guidelines.

With four-color readability, it's great for home use, businesses or churches.

Inside Boot Camp
$15 + $3 shipping and handling

A one-hour audio cassette detailing Jim Paris's most popular strategies — from obtaining low-interest-rate credit cards to investing with no commission. A must for the beginner!

Lighten Your Pack
$15 + $3 shipping and handling

A Christian's guide to lowering tax burdens morally, ethically and legally. One-hour audio cassette.

Paris Perspective Newsletter
$49 per year

Now *you* can stay on the cutting edge of personal finance with the new *Paris Perspective* newsletter. Every month Jim Paris will provide you with his insights on topics such as mutual fund investing and getting the best deal on a new car.

If you are a concerned Christian consumer looking for an "edge" in finance and investment, then the *Paris Perspective* is for you.

Special Forces Training — Credit and Debt
$11.95 + $3 shipping and handling

Jim Paris has compiled a program for Christian consumers who are struggling with debt or bad credit. Three one-hour audio tapes plus two books — Pearl Polto's *Easy Guide to Good Credit* and Marc Eisenson's *The Banker's Secret* — provide you with the proper tools to lower debt effectively and repair bad or nonexistent credit ratings.